D1516313

THE TEXAS RANGER

THE TE★AS RANGER

A Western Duo

Leslie Scott

Five Star • Waterville, Maine

First Edition
First Printing: November 2005

Published in 2005 in conjunction with Golden West Literary Agency.

Set in 11 pt. Plantin by Al Chase.

Printed in the United States on permanent paper.

Library of Congress Cataloging-in-Publication Data

Scott, Leslie, 1893–1975.
    [Drums of doom]
    The Texas ranger : a western duo / by Leslie Scott.—1st ed.
      p. cm.
    "Five Star western"—T.p. verso.
    ISBN 1-59414-163-0 (hc : alk. paper)
    1. Texas Rangers—Fiction. 2. Texas—Fiction. I. Scott, Leslie, 1893–1975. Lone Star peril. II. Title.
PS3537.C9265D78 2005
  813'.52—dc22   2005021492

THE TE★AS RANGER

Table of Contents

Drums of Doom

I

Hanging in a sky of silver-spangled velvet, a red moon brooded over the Maravilla Hills. It was a bloody moon, sullen and menacing, low above the topmost crags that shot upward like teeth in a festering jaw bone. Its mottled face glowered at the grim hills, which seemed to glower back in dark defiance at its lurid light that sought, in vane, to penetrate the ominous gorges already filled by the moan and mutter of white water. It was a moon fit to light the obscene orgies of witches and warlocks, of spectral elementals and goblins.

Pouring into Lost Valley, which was battlemented on the east and west by the beetling cliffs of the Maravillas, the moonlight assumed the quality of a luminous shadow. In its lurid glow, spire rock and chimney rock appeared to crouch and shudder. The crooked branches of mesquite writhed as if in torment. Objects became distorted and unreal, deceptive as to bulk and distance.

Suddenly the silence that brooded over hill and valley was broken by a singular, deep throbbing. Rhythmic and solemn, it shook the night air. A high staccato rattle, from far to the north, was followed after a pause by a deep roll from the south. The deep beat quickened, slowed, then heightened into obvious question and answer.

Riding the rimrock trail on the east wall of the valley, a horseman reined in his black mount to listen. Motionless, he sat for minutes, the concentration furrow deepening between his dark brows, while the air quivered to the ominous throb

11

and mutter that, it seemed to him, monotonously repeated a sentence.

We will kill you if we can! it seemed to say. *We will kill you, if we can!* Over and over, the rumbling threat.

We will kill you, if we can! said the men in the south.

We will kill you, if we can! said the men in the north.

"Indian drums, Shadow, or I never heard one," the rider told his black horse. "War drums, from the sound of them. But what in blazes! Geronimo and his Apache raiders just aren't any more, and there hasn't been any Indian trouble in this section for years. Drums. Talking drums. Shore wish I could read what they're saying."

For a little longer the drums grumbled and muttered. Then the sound died away in a final long roll from the south, echoed by an answering whisper from the north. Again there was eerie silence, broken only by the yipping of a distant coyote, and a vicious reply from an owl nearby.

The tall rider hitched to a more comfortable position the small guitar case suspended across his shoulders. He gathered up the reins, spoke again to the black horse. The clicking iron shoes sounded abnormally loud in the stillness as he started up.

Then, abruptly, the silence that walled in the sounds of the jogging horse was again broken. A distant, wisping clatter grew to a mutter, a beat, a low thunder. The rider straightened in his saddle, stared down into the shadowy valley from which the sound arose.

Suddenly, a few hundred yards to the west, a straggle of chaparral sent forth movement. From behind a jut of chimney rock, too, dimly seen shapes appeared. They moved swiftly northward toward the distant mouth of the valley.

"Cows," the watcher muttered. "Purty good-sized herd, too, and goin' like the wind."

The herd flowed past his range of vision. Behind the galloping steers came mounted men—seven altogether—flapping slickers, snapping quirts, lashing the cattle with rope ends. Then they were gone behind a bristle of growth. The rumble of the speeding herd faded, died away.

But the silence did not resume. Flung out of the south, like a misplaced echo of the drumming hoofs, came a stutter of shots. They were followed by more evenly spaced shots, as if the unseen gunmen were carefully lining on a diminishing target.

Again the horseman pulled up. He shook his black head, listened intently. There was no sound of hoofs clattering toward him, no jingling of bridle iron swelling rhythmically out of the dark.

"Not headed this way," he muttered. "Figgered at first that gunslingin' might have something to do with that herd larrupin' down this way, but I reckon not. Well, this is getting to be quite a night. June along, Shadow, and let's see what's next."

The horseman rode a half mile, and his attention was attracted by a red glow slowly climbing up the southern sky, to the west. The moon, which had risen some distance above the mountain wall, had lost much of its bloody hue now, and its light was changing to ashen silver, shimmering and softening the valley floor. But this new radiance was fierce and fiery.

The tall rider spoke to his horse and the animal quickened his gait.

"That's a house burning or my name's not Slade," the rider declared. "Sift sand, you jughead, let's find out what's goin' on in this section."

The rimrock trail was plain in the moonlight now, and the black horse flashed along it like an ebon shadow. His tall rider leaned forward in the saddle, peering intently at the widening

13

and deepening fire glow. To his ears came a faint sound of shouting. The trail veered around a bulge of stone.

An exciting scene met his gaze as he rounded that curve. Directly ahead, the cliff that formed the east wall of the valley changed to a steep and boulder-strewn slope. Opposite it, a quarter of a mile out on the valley floor, a good-size ranch house was burning fiercely. Flames were shooting from the roof and billowing from the lower windows. In the red light figures ran wildly about.

As the rider reined his horse down, several of those figures ran toward the house with a ladder. They placed it against the ledge of a second-story window. But from a first-floor window, flames shot forth and curled around the lower portion of the ladder. The fierce heat drove back the man who was trying to mount.

A second man tried, only to fail. The figures retreated, shouting and gesturing.

The rider on the rimrock gathered up his reins. His lean, bronzed face grew stern and bleak, and the clear gray of the eyes changed to the wintry chill of a glacier lake.

"I figger we can make it down the slope, feller," he said to his horse. "Looks like somebody's in trouble down there, and no time to waste. Get goin'!"

The horse didn't like the steep slope, and said so with an explosive snort, but he started down it. Slade steadied him with voice and hand. The black animal reached the valley floor in a cloud of dust and a shower of displaced fragments, sitting on his tail. He skittered, but recovered his balance by a miracle of agility.

"Trail, Shadow!" Slade's voice rang out. "Trail!"

Instantly the black extended himself. He flashed across the valley floor like a cloud before a driving wind. Eyes gleaming, nostrils flaring redly, hoofs thundering, he closed the distance, slithering to a halt in the yard of the burning ranch house.

Men shouted wildly and ducked for cover as the great black crashed into their midst. Slade was already out of the saddle.

"What's goin' on here?" his voice rang out, edged with authority. "Why are you tryin' to get that ladder up?"

"The Old Man!" a babble of excited voices answered him. "He's up there . . . second floor . . . saw him at the window . . . smoke got him . . . fell back before he could climb out."

Slade glanced up at the window from which at that moment the ladder, burned in two, dropped with a clatter. He measured the distance with his eye. The flames bursting from the lower window were climbing the outer wall but were still below the second story. Back of the open second-story window, a reddish glow was beginning to strengthen.

"Fire eatin' through the floor," Slade muttered. "Stairs blocked. No tree close enough to climb up and swing in from."

He whirled and gripped the shoulder of a man who seemed somewhat less excited than the rest.

"Get me a crowbar or a post-hole digger," he ordered. "Or even a spade with a long, strong handle."

There was that in his voice which forbade question or argument. The man raced to a small outbuilding nearby and returned with a long-handled spade.

A glance told Slade that the stout handle was of seasoned hickory. He had already taken his rope from his saddle. He noosed the spade handle in the middle now, took a turn and a hitch, and drew it tight. Then he held the spade up, poised over his shoulder.

For an instant he stood rigidly, like a bronze statue of a javelin thrower. Then his long right arm shot forward. The spade hurtled through the air, kept straight by its heavy metal head, the rope trailing behind. Right through the second-story window it shot, to land on the floor with a clatter that sounded above the roar of the flames.

Slade drew the dangling rope taut, whipping the sag up before the flames from the lower window could sear it. As he had figured, the long handle of the spade caught on either side of the window frame and held fast.

Instantly the trained roping horse threw his weight against the rope, tightening it till it hummed. Slade gripped the taut line with sinewy fingers and started up it hand over hand.

Shouts of protest and warning went up from the assembled cowboys.

"Feller, you'll get caught up there and roasted, too."

"The fire'll burn the rope through and you can't git back."

"The Old Man's suffocated by now, anyhow."

Slade heard Shadow snort, and the scrape of his slipping hoofs, but he knew the great black would never slacken the rope. Now he was dangling over the flame-spouting window. Its furnace breath seared him. For an instant his brain whirled, his senses reeled. Then he gripped the window ledge, drew himself up, and with a plunge and heave sprawled on the floor.

Flames flickered through the floor, near the far wall. Their ominous roar and crackle were just outside the closed door. The door itself creaked and groaned under the beat of the fire rushing up from the furnace below. Once the door gave under the strain, a volcano of destruction would pour into the room.

For a moment, Slade lay gasping in the clearer air near the floor. Then he raised himself to hands and knees. An eternity of frantic groping and his hands encountered a limp body. He held the man's pulse and found its thready beat.

"Mebbe we'll make it yet, feller," he muttered.

He whipped the kerchief from his neck, found the man's wrists, and bound them firmly together. Then he stood up, gasping in the heat, and looped the bound arms about his neck. The man was a heavy burden, but he was inches shorter than Slade.

Awkwardly Slade shuffled to the window. Gripping his burden with one arm, he inched onto the sill until he was in a sitting position, his legs dangling down the wall, his boots crisping in the flames licking their soles. He gripped the rope with both hands and moved off the ledge.

"If you slip or take a step now, it's the big jump, feller," he muttered.

But Shadow didn't slip. He snorted loudly as the double weight strained the rope. Irons gripping the ground, legs widespread, he reared back and stood rigidly. The cinch creaked, the saddle tree groaned. But the hull stayed together, and the girth held.

It seemed to Slade that for an age he hung over the blistering flames, his lungs bursting for air, his arms aching with the strain that every instant threatened to tear his hands from their grip and hurl him and his helpless burden into the furnace beneath. The slant of the rope was not enough to permit him to slide down.

Hand over hand, he passed out of reach of the flames. The ground was still a long way off. To let go now meant a broken leg, at least, for himself, possibly death for the unconscious man. His muscles were trembling. His hands felt as if a red-hot iron was being passed back and forth across the palms. An ever-tightening band was around his chest, suffocating him, sapping his strength. Dimly he heard the sound of excited shouts seemingly far below. Then suddenly hands gripped his legs. With a gasp of relief he let go his hold.

The rescuing hands broke his fall. He felt the strangling

arms of the unconscious man plucked from around his neck, the heavy drag of his body removed. Hands lifted him to a sitting position. Somebody pressed a bottle to his lips.

"Son," a voice declared, "you and the Old Man are both livin' on borrowed time."

II

Slade's head quickly cleared. Assisted, he stood up. Behind him sounded a protesting snort.

"Ease off, Shadow," he flung over his shoulder to the black.

"The hoss don't need to," said the man who had spoken. "Rope just burned through and fell down. Son, that was the damnedest smartest piece of work I ever seed."

Slade smiled down at him, his even teeth flashing startlingly white in his bronzed face. "I dunno," he said. "Figgered I had to get in that window somehow, and haven't sprouted wings yet. Calculated a rope was the only way to do it by. It worked."

"It shore did," said the other, "and the Old Man has got you to thank for not wakin' up with a coal shovel in his hands. How is he?" he called to the cowboys who were ministering to the ranch owner.

"Comin' out of it," came the reply. "Be settin' up cussin' in another minute."

The questioner held out his hand.

"Son, my name's Blakely . . . Tom Blakely," he said. "I'm foreman of this spread, the CH, and the old man you saved is the owner, Cal Higborn."

"My name's Slade . . . first handle whittled down to Walt." He shook the proffered hand. "But what's this all about? How'd the fire catch?"

Blakely let loose a string of crackling oaths. "Didn't

19

catch," he growled. "Was set . . . set in half a dozen places on the first floor. A fire arrow or somethin' was shot onto the roof, too. When we heard the noise, and tumbled out of the bunkhouse, the house was blazin' all over. We throwed lead at a coupla sidewinders hightailin' it away from here."

"But who would want to set it?" Slade asked.

Blakely swore some more, and shook his fist at the shadowy south.

"Them god-damned Injuns, who else?"

"Indians? You mean there's Indians raidin' up from Mexico?"

Blakely shook his head. "They live down at the head of the valley," he replied. "Where they always lived. Claim to own the land. Everythin's contrary-wise in this damned section. Injuns ownin' land! An' all the land sloping to the head instead of to the mouth of the valley! Shore the Injuns set the fire. The other day we caught one of the damned bucks snoopin' around on our spread and give him a prime hidin'. This is their way of gettin' even."

"Fellers taking the law in their own hands usually make for trouble," Slade remarked. "Got any real proof the Indians set this fire?"

"Nope," Blakely admitted reluctantly. "You never can prove anythin' on a Injun. The Old Man had a row with old Chief Mukwarrah over some unbranded stock a few months back, and there's been trouble hereabouts ever since. Plenty of stock has been wide-looped."

"Any proof the Indians wide-looped it?" Slade asked.

"There I gotcha," Blakely replied triumphantly. "Nobody seed 'em do it and lived to tell about it, an' nobody found the beefs. But the only way you can run lifted steers outta this valley is south. There ain't a place, east or west, you can run 'em up through the hills. And there's a town at the mouth of the valley it's plumb impossible to get a herd past without bein' spotted. The only way to avoid Concho is to go across the Injun range. Which means the Injuns must've lifted the stock, or was in cahoots with whoever did."

"Sounds reasonable," Slade admitted. "But still you haven't got proof that would stand up in a court of law."

"It won't have to stand up in a court by the time we're done with them hellions," Blakely promised grimly. "Say, I'll betcha while you was ridin' this way you heard drums."

Slade nodded.

"I knowed it," Blakely exulted. "Every time those low snakes cook up some deviltry, they beat those drums. They was heard early the night the Block A lost cows. And when the Walkin' Y lost part of their shippin' herd, they beat the night before. And when Baldy Yates of the Camp Kettle was dry-gulched, they beat the very same night. That's prime proof the Injuns set this burnin', if you heard drums."

A sputter of curse words told that old Cal Higborn had regained his senses. A few minutes later the CH owner got to his feet and hobbled over to thank Slade.

Higborn was a stocky, bristly-whiskered oldster pointedly at variance with his lanky, clean-shaven foreman. With an old border-campaigner's efficiency, he immediately took charge of the situation.

"The ranch house is a goner," he growled, glaring with truculent blue eyes at the flame-spouting structure. "But there's plenty of sleepin' room in the bunkhouse. We got some Dutch ovens and an old range in the stable. We can set 'em up to cook on. Plenty of pots and pans in there, too. See the storehouse didn't ketch, so we don't go short on chuck. We'll hafta sorta camp out till we can build a new *casa*. We'll start on that soon as the ashes cool on them foundations."

At his orders, the cowpunchers went to work, setting up an

improvised kitchen in the front part of the big barn. By the time they had completed his further orders, the fire was well on the way to burning itself out. Up until that time, Slade and two others kept a sharp watch on the roofs of the barn and other outbuildings on the chance that a stray brand might fire them, also.

"Well, I reckon that's all we can do tonight," Higborn announced at length. "Figger we might as well grab a mite of shut-eye 'fore come mornin'. Things 'pear to be quietin' down."

But as the men headed for the bunkhouse, a clatter of hoofs sounded on the night air. The hoofs drummed swiftly louder, and a sweat-lathered horse flashed from the south, into the circle of the firelight. A wild-eyed cowboy rocked and reeled in the saddle. His face was stiff with caked blood and he appeared in the last stages of exhaustion.

"It's Harley Bell!" somebody yelled. "What in tarnation's the matter with you, Harley?"

The injured man was helped from his saddle, and steadied on his feet. He stared dazedly at the still burning ruin of the ranch house.

"The shippin' herd we was gettin' together," he mumbled finally. "She's gone . . . wide-looped. Purdy's dead . . . head bashed in. Must've hit me a glancin' blow . . . or I'd be dead, too."

"What in blazes are you gabbin' about?" bellowed old Cal. "Shake yourself together."

"Hellions slipped up on me and Purdy," Bell managed. "We was ridin' herd, and met under a tree while makin' our rounds. The tree set on the edge of brush. It was dark, with a blasted red moon seemin' to make it darker. I heard Purdy grunt, and I turned to see what was the matter, and somethin' hit me over the head. When I come to, the herd was gone.

Purdy was layin' on the ground with the whole back of his head caved in. Happened not long after dark."

"It's past midnight now," somebody said.

"Them hellions got several hours' start, then," Bell mumbled.

"And before we could get after them, they'd be out through the head of the valley and well on the way to *mañana* land," Higborn remarked grimly. "Take Bell in, and wash his head and plaster it. Nothin' we can do tonight."

Again the cowboys headed for the bunkhouse, chattering angrily, and profanely blaming the Indians at the head of the valley.

But Walt Slade, who the *peónes* of the river villages named El Halcón—The Hawk—recalled a shadowy herd of cattle fleeing madly through the red light of a bloody moon, and was silent. The concentration furrow was once more deep between his black brows.

III

Morning found the CH cowboys astir early. After quantities of
steaming coffee, and a hot breakfast that the cook had thrown
together on the old range in the barn, several of the men rode
out to bring in the body of Purdy, the slain cowpuncher. Old Cal
Higborn called Slade aside.

"You got the look of a top hand about you, son," he said.
"I lost a good rider last night, and that leaves me one short.
There's a job open here if you'd care to sign on."

"I've a notion I will hang around for a spell," Slade replied
thoughtfully. "Reckon you've hired a hand."

"Fine," said Higborn. "I'm ridin' to town now to let the
sheriff know what happened. You can ride with me and look
the range over on the way."

A wrangler brought the horses around, and they set out.

"It's four hours of good ridin'," Higborn said. "We oughta
make it by noon. But don't go lettin' that black of yours out.
I've a notion there ain't many cayuses can stay nose to nose
with him if he's in a hurry."

"Old Shadow can step a mite if he takes a notion," Slade
admitted. "Say, this is nice-looking range."

"It is good, when things are runnin' smooth," Higborn
said. "Good grass, plenty of water. Cañons in the hills for
shelter from sun and snow. With the right sort of neighbors,
you'd be settin' pretty. But so long as them Injuns hold the
head of the valley. . . ." He trailed off into profane rumblings.

Slade, gazing across the emerald billows of grass, dotted

24

with thickets and groves and walled east and west by tall cliffs, was silent and thoughtful. He recalled Blakely's remark, of the night before, that the general slope of the land was toward the head of the valley rather than its mouth. The hill-locked valley was unusual in other ways. He estimated its width at thirty miles, the western cliffs being hazy with distance. The trail they were following, he noticed, veered steadily to the west in its northward trend.

Section looks like it all of a sudden dropped down hundreds of feet sometime a million years back, he mused. *But even after ages of wear, those cliffs are still torn and ragged. No signs of a big stream having run here to cut the valley down through the hills, either. Wonder just what did bring it about?*

Slade, before the murder of his father by wide-loopers and the subsequent loss of the elder Slade's prosperous ranch that set him to riding the dim trails that bordered outlawry, had had three years in a famous college of engineering. He was interested in geological formations. In the years that followed the interruption of his college training, he had kept up his studies after a fashion, and he knew more about geology than many a man who could write a degree after his name.

He was recalled to the present by old Cal's rumbling voice. Higborn was veering his horse into a track that cut the main trail at a sharp angle. They had been riding some two hours and had covered about half the distance to the town at the valley mouth.

"Over west a mile is the Block O ranch house," said Higborn. "I wanna stop and see Blaine Ollendorf a minute. Blaine owns the spread and is a pretty good feller."

As they rode into the yard of the ranch house, a man came out onto the porch to greet them.

"Hi, Blaine!" shouted Higborn. "Want a word with you."

Ollendorf was a big, massively built man with abnormally

long and thick arms. A mane of tawny hair swept back from his broad brow and curled low at the back of his head. There were dark rings below his eyes, however, and the eyes themselves were bloodshot, Slade noted.

"What brings you down this way so early, Cal?" Ollendorf asked.

"Headin' for town to see the sheriff," Higborn replied. "Wanna come along?"

Ollendorf shook his head. "Was to town yesterday," he said. "Got back just about dark and went right to bed. Was plumb tuckered out. Got up just a while ago. Wanna ride up to my south range soon as I've had a bite to eat. Join me in a helpin'?"

"We et early," Higborn replied. "I'll tell you what happened over to my place last night."

He regaled the Block O owner with a vividly profane account of the previous night's occurrences. Ollendorf clucked sympathetically, shaking his square head.

"And if it hadn't been for Slade here, I wouldn't be tellin' you about it," concluded Higborn. "I was sound asleep in my room upstairs when the shoutin' outside woke me up. I was all groggy with smoke. The room was full of it. I managed to get to the door and open it. Fire was roaring up the stairs and along the hall. Had sense enough to shut the door, but that was about all. Tried to get to the window. Couldn't breathe. Couldn't see. Felt myself goin'. Never did get to the window. Next thing I knowed, I was layin' on the ground with the boys workin' over me. They told me what Slade had done, just like I told you. Yeah, I owe him plenty. Want you to know him. Shake hands with Blaine Ollendorf, Slade."

Ollendorf glanced keenly at The Hawk, an inscrutable look in his dark eyes as they shook hands.

"Plumb glad to know you," he acknowledged heartily.

"I'd have felt mighty bad if anythin' had happened to Cal. Mighty lucky you happened along so handy. You say you're ridin' in to see Sheriff Fanshaw?" he asked Higborn.

"Uhn-huh. And if Willis don't do somethin' about it *pronto*, I've a mighty good notion to take my boys and ride to the head of the valley and chase them Injuns clean to Mexico."

Ollendorf shook his head. "I wouldn't do that if I was you, Cal," he said. "After all, you got no real proof old Mukwarrah and his bucks fired your ranch house and run off your herd. Suspectin' ain't provin', you know, and you'll find yourself up against the law if you try to run them Injuns off the land they own."

"What right they got to own land?" bellowed Higborn.

"The court over to the capital says they own it fair and square," Ollendorf pointed out. "You know what happened when Baldy Yates tried to prove that land was part of the Camp Kettle spread. The courts said the old Spanish grant by which Mukwarrah got his title was plumb valid, and they upheld Mukwarrah's side of the arguin'."

"But if Baldy hadn't been dry-gulched and left with a slug through his head right after he started the suit, he'd have won out," declared the stubborn Higborn. "Baldy was smart and salty, and he'd have found a way. Mukwarrah knowed that, and that's why he had Baldy dry-gulched."

"No proof that Mukwarrah had anythin' to do with it," objected Ollendorf. "Baldy was plumb salty, as you say, and there was plenty of fellers who had it in for him. He had trouble over in the west *rincón* of the Big Bend before he came here. Folks over in that section are sorta good at holdin' grudges."

Walt Slade took no part in this conversation. He sat perched on the porch railing, swinging one long leg, his eyes fixed thoughtfully on the rusty iron boot scraper nailed to the end of the lowest step, apparently paying no mind whatever to what was said.

"Just the same, if somethin' ain't done *pronto*, I'm ridin' to visit Mukwarrah," finished Higborn. "And," he added grimly, "I won't have no trouble with the law afterwards, 'cause there won't be no witnesses against me. I've stood just about all I'm gonna stand."

Ollendorf changed the subject. "By the way," he said, "do you need lumber to rebuild with? I got a coupla stacks you can have. Had quite a lot left when I finished my new barns. It'll save you a haul from Concho."

"That's just what I wanted to see you about," admitted Higborn. "It's mighty nice of you, Blaine. I'll send the wagons over tomorrow. Be seein' you."

Ollendorf nodded good bye to Slade, as they turned to go. "Drop in any time you're ridin' hereabouts."

"Blaine's a mighty accommodatin' feller, even if he is loco where them Injuns is concerned," remarked old Cal as they rode back to the main trail.

Slade nodded, but made no comment.

The day had turned hot, and they rode more slowly now. An hour passed and they had covered somewhat less than the remaining distance to Concho, at the mouth of the valley. The trail had been constantly veering westward and now they were but a slight distance from the valley's precipitous west slopes.

Higborn kept up a constant chatter and was heedless of his surroundings, but Slade spoke seldom, and his eyes were searching every thicket and jut of chimney rock they passed. During his years of riding furtive trails, Walt Slade had learned to be watchful, particularly in a section where there were inexplicable happenings. And now, in a corner of his

28

brain, a silent monitor was setting up a clamor. Slade had learned to heed that unheard voice, and had before now profited from its warnings.

Higborn was still grumbling about the Indians of Lost Valley. Abruptly his growling monotone was cut off as Slade's long arm swept him from the saddle and sent him crashing to the ground. Almost before he landed, Slade was beside him, crouched low, his heavy Winchester in his hands.

The long barrel flung up, and lined on a puff of smoke that at that instant wisped from bushes some distance up the slope. Even as a bullet screamed over the startled horses' backs, Higborn saw Slade squeeze trigger, and fire spurted from the black muzzle of the saddle gun. The crash of the report was an echo to the one slamming down from the slope.

The growth on the slope was violently agitated for a moment, then was still. There was no further evidence of movement in the veiling brush.

"Keep down," Slade's voice warned. "If I just winged him and he's still able to fang, we'll hear from him again if he manages to line with us."

For long moments they lay rigidly, eyes fixed on the growth. Slade estimated the distance to a straggle of thicket on the valley floor at the base of the slope.

"I've a notion I can make it," he muttered. "If I can, I oughta be able to creep up the slope and mebbe get in back of the sidewinder, if he's still there. Worth a try, anyhow."

With the words he was on his feet, crouching low, zigzagging to the thickets. But even as he dived into its shelter, a figure crashed into the brush alongside of him.

"Think I'm gonna hole up there like a gopher while you make a try for that hyderphobia skunk?" old Cal demanded indignantly. "I was a scout and doin' border fightin' before you was born. We're in this together."

"OK." Slade chuckled, smiling down at the flushed face of the angry old-timer. "Take it easy, now, if you're comin' with me. If he's still up there and locates us, we're liable for a dose of lead poisoning before we can line sights on him."

He quickly realized, however, that old Cal could move through the brush as silently as himself. Slowly they wormed their way up the slope until Slade decided they were slightly higher than the spot from where the shot had come. Then they diagonalled to the south.

Abruptly Slade laid a restraining hand on his companion's arm. Only a few yards distant was something huddled beneath a bush. They crept toward it, but the form remained motionless.

A moment later they were standing over it, guns ready.

"Done in, all right," Slade said.

"Shore is," Higborn agreed, jerking his thumb toward the black hole between the dead man's staring eyes. "You drilled him dead center, son. How in blazes did you come to see him?"

"Saw the sunlight glint on his rifle barrel when he shifted it," Slade replied. "Had a notion this slope might bear a mite of watching. It's perfect for a dry-gulchin' of anybody riding the trail down there."

Old Cal peered at the face of the dead dry-gulcher, uncertainly seen in the shadow. Suddenly he swore an exultant oath.

"What'd I tell you?" he barked. "Look . . . it's a Injun, one of old Mukwarrah's Yaqui bucks, shore as you're a foot high."

El Halcón squatted beside the dead man, examining the distorted face with calculating eyes. The dry-gulcher was undoubtedly an Indian. He was dark, with a broad, evil-looking face. His mouth was a wide slit, his nose flaring and fleshy.

He wore his straight black hair in a bank across his low fore-head.

Slade turned to the chortling Higborn.

"You say Mukwarrah and his bucks are Yaquis?"

"Uhn-huh." Higborn nodded. "Every one of 'em. Come up from *Méjico* originally. Ornery mountain Yaquis, that's what they are. Well, they can't worm out of this one. This is one time those hellions is caught with the smooth-iron hot."

Slade stared curiously at the dead man's lank hair. Now he turned again to Higborn.

"Cal," he said, as he straightened up, "I don't like to mention it, but last night I sorta did you a favor."

"You shore did," old Cal agreed emphatically.

"Well," said The Hawk, "I'd sorta like to ask you to do me one in turn."

"I promise even afore you ask," Higborn instantly answered. "Anythin' you ask. Half my spread, if you want it."

"Wouldn't know what to do with it, if I had it." Slade smiled. "What I want you to promise is not to say anything to anybody about what happened here this morning, until I give the word."

Old Cal stared at him. "I shore don't know what you're drivin' at," he sputtered, "and it sounds plumb loco to me, but I've passed my word, and I ain't never broke it yet."

"OK," Slade agreed. "Now, let's see what this hellion has in his pockets. Might tell us something about him."

The contents of the dead man's pockets, however, held no significance. Slade appeared neither surprised nor disappointed.

"His horse oughta be somewhere around," he commented. "Mebbe we can find it."

They finally did locate the horse tethered in a dense thicket. It was a shaggy-coated, unkempt animal, unshod and

31

unbranded. The rig was plain and bore no trademark.

Again Slade did not appear surprised. Without comment he got the trappings off the animal and turned it loose to graze.

"Can take care of itself, I figger," he told Higborn. "About half wild, as it is. Chances are it'll take up with some wild herd in the hills. There are probably plenty of that sort hereabouts."

"There are," agreed Higborn. "Gonna leave this feller lie?"

"For the present, anyhow," Slade replied.

"Reckon the buzzards will take care of him," Higborn predicted cheerfully.

"Yes," Slade agreed with peculiar emphasis, "I expect the buzzards *will* take care of him."

IV

The interview with Sheriff Willis Fanshaw in Concho proved to be a stormy one. Higborn stated his grievances and demanded justice. Sheriff Fanshaw was willing to oblige, but didn't see his way clear just how to go about it.

"I'll get a posse together and comb the hills for your cows," he told the rancher, "but I can't go ridin' to Mukwarrah and accuse him of liftin' 'em, not without proof."

"Damned lot of chance you'd have of findin' 'em now," Higborn replied caustically. "Them cows are plumb to Mexico, and you know it. But if you don't do somethin' *pronto*, I'm gonna do some ridin' myself."

The sheriff flushed, and tugged at his mustache.

"Takin' the law in your own hands won't get you anythin', Cal," he said. "Besides, last week I wrote Captain Jim McNelty over to Ranger headquarters to send along a troop to keep order in this section if necessary. You don't hanker to buck McNelty's men, do you, Cal?"

"McNelty ain't got no troop of Rangers to send here right now, and you know it." Higborn nodded his head for emphasis. "He's plumb busy down along the Big Bend border, and with them Bast outlaws what have been raisin' the devil over New Mexico way. Besides," he added shrewdly, "he'll tell you it's a matter for the local authorities to take care of, which it is. Betcha you ain't got no answer to your letter."

The sheriff had to admit that he had not. Old Cal chortled derisively.

After leaving the sheriff's office, Slade and Higborn repaired to a saloon for a drink and chuck. While they were eating, two men entered and approached their table. Higborn greeted them as old acquaintances, and introduced Slade.

"This is Andy Ballou of the Walkin' F, and Thankful Yates, who owns the Camp Kettle," he introduced them to Slade. "Thankful come over from Arizona and took charge after his brother, Baldy Yates, was dry-gulched. You heard me speak to Blaine Ollendorf about Baldy this mornin', Slade."

Andy Ballou was corpulent and cheerful. Yates was tall and thin. He had a hard face, a tight mouth, and calculating gray eyes. He packed two guns, and his movements were lithe and furtive. With a single swift, appraising glance he took in the broad-shouldered, lean-waisted Hawk from head to foot. His gaze lingered a moment on the two heavy black guns hung low in carefully oiled and worked cut-out holsters from double cartridge belts. His handshake was firm and cordial.

Ballou swore as old Cal outlined his misfortunes of the night before. Yates, evidently a taciturn individual, offered no comment other than a nod of his red head. Both invited Slade to drop in if he happened to ride in the neighborhood of their ranch houses.

"Thankful is the black sheep of the Yates family, I reckon," Higborn observed as they headed back for the CH. "Baldy was just sorta gray-colored. Thankful got into a shootin' down in the Big Bend a few years back and had to light out till things cooled down. Was in Arizona when Baldy got killed. Came back to take over the Camp Kettle. Seemed sorta sobered and has behaved hisself since he was here. He's pizen with them two guns, though, I'm told."

Slade went to work for the CH, and quickly won the approval of both Blakely, the foreman, and the hands. Soon

Blakely assigned him to the difficult and dangerous work of combing strays from the brakes and cañons of the west range. This was work to El Halcón's liking, for it gave him time for some investigations of his own. He spent much time in the gorges and cañons, examining them in the minutest detail.

One afternoon, beyond the south limits of the CH range, he was riding slowly along not far from the west wall of the valley. He was about to push through a fringe of thicket, when his eye caught something going on some distance ahead. Reining Shadow in, still in the concealment of the thicket, he lounged in the saddle and watched curiously the activities of a group of men who sat their horses under a large tree. Slade counted eight altogether.

As he watched, all but one of the men wheeled their horses and rode swiftly toward the western slope. The one re-mained, sitting his horse under the tree.

Slade watched the group until it vanished into the brush of the slope. Then his gaze returned to the single horseman, who still sat stiffly erect in the shade of the tree. His horse stood motionlessly, save for an occasional impatient stamp of a hoof or a switch of its tail.

Is that jigger posing for a picture, or something? Slade mused. *Hasn't moved an inch since the others left.*

He spoke to Shadow and rode slowly toward the motion-less man, casting an occasional glance toward the slope that had swallowed his companions.

Still the man did not move. He sat lance-straight on his horse, staring straight ahead of him, his hands apparently resting on the pommel of the saddle.

As he drew nearer, Slade made out what looked like a thin black line running from the man's head to a branch of the tree. A little nearer, and suddenly he stiffened.

"Blazes," he muttered, "of all the devilish things to do."

He swore under his breath as he realized the fiendishness
of the thing. It was a savage refinement of cruelty. The black
line was a rope. One end was noosed about the man's neck.
The other was fastened to the tree branch overhead. Slade
could now see that his hands were bound in front of him. He
was all set for a hanging, and hanged he would be, despite the
departure of his executioners. For the horse was not tied. Let
it take a step forward and the man would be dragged from the
saddle and left dangling by his neck. There he must sit,
awaiting with nerves tortured to exquisite agony the inevitable happening. He might be able to keep the horse still with
his voice for a while, but sooner or later the animal, driven by
hunger or thirst or some wayward impulse, was bound to
move.

Slade was in a quandary. Any minute the horse might
move. If he approached slowly, he might be too far off to
reach the victim in time to save him, should the horse take a
step. If he urged Shadow to speed, his approach might
frighten the animal and cause it to run. After a swift calculation of the risks, he resolved on the former course.

Step by step the black horse moved forward. Slade could
see the forward pricking ears of the other animal as it focused
its gaze on the approaching black. It stamped nervously,
tossed its head. The helpless man's lips moved. He was
doubtless talking to his mount in low tones, endeavoring to
allay its nervousness.

Slade was still several hundreds yards distant. The horse
under the tree was showing more and more nervousness.
Once it moved a little, and the dangling rope tightened. The
man strained his head back to ease the pressure on his throat.
His helpless fingers twitched spasmodically.

Step by slow step. El Halcón's face was bleak as the
granite of the glowering cliffs. His eyes were cold as water

under frozen snow. One slender hand dropped to the black butt of a gun.

The victim's horse was plainly frightened by the slow advance. Slade felt Shadow shiver as the other horse's nervousness was communicated to him.

The victim's horse raised a forehoof, stamped, twitched its tail, tossed its head. And still 100 yards to go. The horse snorted, blowing prodigiously through its flaring nostrils. Slade saw its muscles tensed. And fifty yards yet to go!

The frightened horse snorted again. It plunged forward, went careening off across the range. Its rider was jerked from the saddle and left dangling in mid-air, his body writhing, his legs kicking convulsively.

Instantly Slade's hand flashed down and up. Clamped tightly against his sinewy hip, the long black gun spouted flame. The reports blended in a veritable drum roll of sound as the Hawk shot at the rope.

Swiftly he counted the shots. One—two—three—four.

The Colt was rock-steady; he hesitated an instant on that last shot remaining, and squeezed the trigger. He gave a gasp of relief as the writhing body dropped through the air and thudded on the ground. The severed end of the rope snapped sharply up amid the branches.

"Trail, Shadow!" Slade's voice rang out. "Trail!"

The great black shot forward with the speed of light. Slade went out of the saddle with the mount still going at full gallop. He dropped beside the prostrate man and with frantic fingers ripped the tight noose from his swollen neck.

The man's face was black with congested blood. The veins on his forehead stood out big as cords. But the man's heart was still going, his lungs working. Gasping and retching, he fought for breath. The blood drained from his face, his lids fluttered. A moment later they raised, and steady black eyes stared up at Slade.

The man was an Indian. His face was aquiline and finely featured, although it was a network of wrinkles. His hair, hanging in a straight bang across his broad and high forehead, was white as mountain snow. His mouth was well formed and kindly.

"Take it easy, old-timer," Slade said. "Get your breath back and rest a mite. You came mighty nigh to makin' the happy huntin' grounds that time."

The old man lay motionlessly for a few minutes, his unwinking black eyes still regarding the face of his rescuer. Then, with the assistance of Slade's arm, he raised himself to a sitting position.

"Mukwarrah thanks you," he said.

V

Relaxing comfortably on his heels, Slade rolled a cigarette with the slim fingers of his left hand and proffered it to the old chief. Mukwarrah accepted with a nod. Slade rolled another for himself, and the two men smoked silently.

The Hawk's eyes constantly searched the western slope. Mukwarrah read his thoughts with native shrewdness.

"I do not think they will return," he remarked.

"Mebbe not," Slade admitted, "but no use taking chances." He rose, slid his Winchester from the saddle boot, and laid it on the grass beside him.

"It will be greatly to their misfortune if they risk themselves within range of El Halcón's guns," Mukwarrah commented.

Slade shot him a swift glance.

"How come you to know me?" he asked.

"Many know you," the chief returned quietly. "Especially those who are lowly or in need of help. You could be no other. This morning, when I was in the town, I heard people saying El Halcón was riding for the *Señor* Higborn. Who first said it, no one seems to know, but the word is spoken by many now. I knew you not, but none but El Halcón could have shot as you shot when you severed the rope and saved my life."

With a smile, Slade lightly changed the subject.

"You talk mighty good English, Chief," he said.

Mukwarrah nodded. "I was educated in the San Vicente mission across the Río Grande," he said.

"You do talk English more like an educated Mexican than a Texan," Slade agreed.

The old chief stood up, still slightly unsteady on his feet. Slade followed the direction of his glance.

"I'll fetch your horse for you," he offered. "I see he's got over his scare and is grazing over there by the slope."

He caught the horse with little difficulty, and Mukwarrah mounted.

"Will you visit my village?" the Indian invited.

Slade considered a moment, glancing at the sun.

"We can reach the village before it is dark," Mukwarrah said.

"OK."

They rode down the valley.

"How'd those hellions manage to tie onto you?" Slade asked.

"They roped me as I rode near the slope," Mukwarrah explained. "It was cleverly done. I was helpless before I could raise a hand."

"Recognize any of 'em?"

"They wore masks over their faces," the Yaqui replied.

"Happen to get a look at their hands?"

Mukwarrah shot him a quick glance.

"The hands of three were dark," he said.

"And I reckon it was them three that figgered out that cute little hangin' trick." The Hawk nodded. "They're good at that sort of thing."

Mukwarrah nodded grave agreement.

The sun was setting when they reached the site of the Indian village, and in the light of its level rays Slade could see, in the far distance, the narrow gorge leading to the Río Grande and Mexico.

The village, a group of well-built lodges, was set on a little mesa rising considerably above the valley floor. Good crops were growing on cleared land and the range was dotted with grazing cattle. Slade saw numbers of horses and mules, and a fine herd of goats.

"We are peaceful folk here," Mukwarrah observed. "All we ask is to live in peace with our neighbors, and so we did do until recently. Now, we constantly fear trouble. The *Señor* Higborn, and others think ill of us. He thinks we rustle his cattle."

"I've a notion he'll get over that before long," Slade said.

"I hope so." Mukwarrah shook his white head sadly. "The charge is most untrue. My young men do not steal. I have reared them in the faith of the good Fathers of the mission. They obey the laws of their land, for it is their land, as it is the land of the *Señor* Higborn and his friends. They would fight and die for it if necessary."

"I've a plumb notion they would," Slade agreed with warmth. "And I've another notion . . . that the time will come when Higborn and his friends will sit in your lodge as your friends."

The old chief gave him a long look.

"If El Halcón says it is so, then it is so," he remarked simply.

After a bountiful supper in the chief's lodge, Mukwarrah proposed the young men put on a tribal dance for their guest's pleasure. Slade knew that Indians, contrary to popular opinion, were not a solemn and silent people. Here was laughter and gaiety and sociability.

He enjoyed the dance greatly, knowing he was witnessing a spectacle few white men ever saw. One of the Indians owned a guitar, and after the dance was ended, Slade tuned the instrument to his liking and sang in a voice like the wind in the hilltop pines, like the rushing white water in the cañons, gay songs of the range land, and haunting Spanish melodies. His hosts sat spellbound as the great golden baritone-bass pealed and thundered in the light of the late moon.

It was past midnight when the celebration broke up and Slade went to sleep in the chief's lodge.

"Mukwarrah," he said the following morning as he stood beside his saddled horse. "Mukwarrah, is there any other way out of this valley besides across your range or by Concho?"

"Not that I have ever heard of." The chief shrugged. "Not that it is impossible. But there has never been a need for another way out, so why should anybody look for one?"

When Slade reached the CH ranch house in the late afternoon, he found the place in an uproar.

"A big herd was shoved off the Walkin' Y spread last night," Higborn told him.

"And them Injun drums was beatin' again," Tom Blakely added. "I tell you, boss, we gotta do somethin'. I'm scared about the shippin' herd we're gettin' together. I can't keep the boys out there guardin' all the holdin' spots every night. But if we don't, them hellions is sure to run a bunch off. We can't afford to lose any more stock."

"We'll do somethin'," Higborn promised grimly, "and mighty soon."

A little later he drew Slade aside.

"Son," he said, "I was to town to see the sheriff again today. I found Willis pawin' dirt clean over his back. Appears folks there have been tellin' him you are El Halcón. Not that I give a hoot if you're John Wesley Hardin hisself, but I figgered you oughta know about it. I pinned Willis down, an' he admitted he didn't have any warrant for you and didn't know anybody what had. But he said folks allowed if you wasn't a owlhoot, you missed bein' one by the skin of your teeth, and that you had killed more'n one man. I asked him if he ever heard tell of you killin' anybody what didn't have a killin' comin'. He like to swore the shingles off the roof. Then he hedged, and opined it was beside the point, that nobody had any right to take the law in his own hands, and that he had enough trouble as is, without a two-gun killer sashayin' around the section. I allowed there wasn't much he could do about it. By the way, where was you last night?"

"Down in Chief Mukwarrah's village," Slade replied.

Old Cal's jaw dropped, and his eyes goggled.

"For Pete's sake, don't let anybody else know about it," he sputtered. "If folks find out you was with them Injuns when Ballou's herd was wide-looped, they'll. . . ."

"Higborn," Slade interrupted, "that wide-looped herd never went across Mukwarrah's range."

"Then where the . . . ?"

"Mukwarrah's bucks put on a tribal dance for me last night," Slade interrupted again. "The shindig lasted until long past midnight. It was bright starlight in the early evening, with a bright moon later on. No herd could've gone through the gorge and not been seen. All of Mukwarrah's young men were there when the dance busted up, and they were all there early this morning when I left. You'll have to leave Mukwarrah out of this one."

"If you say that, I reckon I'll have to," Higborn admitted. "But if the Injuns didn't do it, who did?"

"That remains to be found out," Slade said. "I'm goin' to pound my ear for a spell. I want to ride over to the west range early tomorrow."

He rode the range very early the following morning. Before daybreak, in fact.

The level rays of the rising sun found him close to the western wall of the valley, riding very slowly northward.

Along the base of the cliffs, his keen gaze intently searched the ground.

Mile after mile he rode, and found nothing. Then, some miles north of the confines of the CH range, where the over-flow of a little spring formed a patch of marshy ground, he came upon a multitude of hoof marks. Here and there, also, were the imprints of horses' irons.

Might be just a bunch stopping here for a drink, he mused, scanning the ground, *but those prints are deep, and splayed out. Looks more like a herd siftin' sand mighty fast. Headed north, too, and the prints don't look very old.*

He rode on, intent and watchful, but the thickly growing grass of the range land was impervious to the marks of passing hoofs. Once, however, his quick glance noted a fresh white score on a slab of rock, the kind of scrape made by the slipping iron of a shod horse.

Several miles more, and in the cliff wall yawned the dark mouth of a narrow cañon. The floor was hard and stony, thinly grown with brush except along the walls. There were signs—cattle had from time to time entered the gorge.

"Not that it means much," the Hawk muttered. "Chances are there's water back in there, and the steers would naturally go for that. Still, some of these marks look fresh."

He turned into the cañon, which slashed the hills in a westerly direction. Soon he discovered there was water in the gorge—a good-size spring gushing from under the rock wall and forming a stream that ran into the depths of the cañon.

Slade's eyes glowed.

Sorta proves my theory about the geological formation of this section, he told himself. *The slope of this cañon is away from the valley, not toward it. I figgered I'd find something like this sooner or later.*

With quickened interest he rode on, following the banks of

the little stream. He had covered three miles when the stream began to broaden and overflow its banks. Soon Shadow was splashing through a small marsh of sticky black mud, grown with rank grasses. Slade's eyes lit up again as they rested on the dark surface of the bog.

The marshy ground was slashed and scored by a multitude of hoof prints.

"Fresh, too," the Hawk said. "Not more'n forty-eight hours old."

The prints led into the gloomy depths of the cañon. Slade followed them, Shadow's hoofs sucking and splashing in the black mud. The stream continued to broaden and shallow. Finally the water vanished altogether, absorbed by the spongy ground, doubtless to drain off by some subterranean channel. The ground began to grow firmer, and farther on was replaced by hard, stony soil upon which the hoofs of the passing herd had left no imprint. For a mile farther Slade rode, then he abruptly reined Shadow in and sat, staring. He swore under his breath with bitter disappointment.

Directly ahead was a sheer rock wall towering up against the blue of the morning sky. The cañon was a box.

"Looks sorta like the nice little house we built is all tumbled down, Shadow," he told the black horse. "A goat couldn't get up that rock, and the side walls all the way in are just as steep. Begins to appear that in here is just a watering spot for stray doggies, after all."

He rolled a cigarette, lighted it, and sat frowning at the blank wall.

"Just the same, those hoof marks back there didn't look like the prints of straying cows," he growled. "Looked a heap more like they were made by a herd being shoved along hard and fast. Has somebody found a way to sprout wings on beefs, or lizard legs? Appears sorta like it."

With a disgusted snort, he turned Shadow's head toward the south wall of the cañon and rode slowly back the way he had come, examining the rock wall for some cleft or fissure he might have missed on his trip into the gorge.

The cliffs reared sheer, with thick, tall chaparral at their base. Slade eyed the growth, searching for signs of the phantom herd having brushed against it in passing. But the close bristle stretched unbroken as the rock wall towered above it.

Abruptly he reined in, his eyes narrowing. The stretch of growth he was just passing stood straight and tall, but there was a withered look about the leaves on the topmost branches, a tinge of yellow at variance with the fresh green on either side. For perhaps a dozen feet this peculiar manifestation was evident.

His eyes glowing with excitement, Slade slipped from the saddle. Through his mind ran stories of owlhoot tricks told by old border peace officers. He approached the growth, broke off a branch of one of the bushes. It snapped sharply in his fingers.

"Dry," he muttered. "Dead and dry."

He stopped, seized the gnarled trunk with both hands, and tugged sharply. The trunk slid easily out of the ground. It had no roots. Its base was a sharpened stake.

Slade tossed the bush aside, seized another. A moment of tugging and he had a gap in the growth a couple of yards in width. Through it shone the cliff wall, and in the wall yawned a dark opening.

VI

Wordlessly Slade stared at the cave mouth. He shoved his wide hat back on his crisp black hair and gave a low whistle.

"An old trick," he exclaimed aloud, "but a good one! Cut out the brush, then stick it back in the ground after you pass through the gap. That way there's no broken branches or tramped down bush. Anybody ridin' through here would never suspect that cave in the cliff. Would never notice the break in the growth unless they were looking mighty sharp and had a good notion what they were looking for. Wouldn't have noticed it myself if those hellions hadn't got careless and neglected to replace the withered bushes with fresh ones. That's the way with the owlhoot breed . . . always overlookin' some mite of a thing. Not much, a few withered leaves, but enough to make a jigger stretch rope. Shadow, I'll bet you a hatful of *pesos* that cave is a tunnel runnin' right straight through the hill and into a gorge or valley on the far side. And in that gorge will be a trail leading south. Let's you and me go and see. Wait a minute, though. It's dark in there, and the going is apt to be rough."

He searched about amid the growth until he found some pieces of dry resinous wood. Lighting one for a torch, he led Shadow to the mouth of the cave.

The sides of the cave were smooth and water-worn, its floor carpeted with fine silt sprinkled with pebbles and small, rounded boulders. Slade nodded with satisfaction.

"Just what I figgered we'd find sooner or later," he said.

"A waterway through the hills. Uhn-huh, that's the old bed of a stream that once ran through here, a mighty long time back, when this section was different from what it is now. And look at the hoof marks in that silt. Plenty of cows been shoved through this hole."

He mounted, and rode into the cave, holding his torch high. Shadow's irons clattered loudly on the boulders, but the floor had a slight slope and was devoid of pitfalls. For a mile, Slade rode through thick darkness that was relieved only by the flickering flame of his torch. Then, suddenly, he saw light ahead.

Five minutes more and he was sitting his horse in the far mouth of the tunnel. Before him stretched a narrow gorge trending in a southerly direction. Down the middle of the gorge ran a trail that showed evidence of recent travel.

"Uhn-huh." He nodded with satisfaction. "This is their private back door to *mañana* land and a market for wide-looped beefs."

With a final glance at the gorge, which flowed southward for as far as his eyes could reach, he turned back into the tunnel. Reaching the cañon once more, he carefully replaced the cut brush, making sure all was as before. Then he rode swiftly to the cañon mouth and headed for the CH ranch house.

Old Cal was working at his desk when Slade entered. He looked up, glowering from under his bushy brows.

"Now what?" he demanded. "Somethin' else bust loose?"

Slade drew up a chair. He was fumbling at a cunningly contrived secret pocket in his broad leather belt. He laid an object on the desk in front of the ranch owner.

Cal Higborn stared, his jaw sagging. The object was a silver star set on a silver circle, the honored, feared, and re-spected badge of the Texas Rangers.

The old rancher gasped.

"A . . . a Ranger! You . . . you're a Ranger?"

"Figger to be." Slade smiled. "Undercover man for Captain Jim McNelty. Captain Jim got Sheriff Fanshaw's letter, and sent me over here to have a look-see at what was going on."

"And you're here to hawg-tie them Injuns!" Higborn crowed happily.

"I'm here to hawg-tie the gents who've been doin' the wide-loopin' and general mischief in this section," Slade corrected with emphasis. He slid the silver badge back into its secret pocket. "Remember, if folks in general knew El Halcón was a Ranger, my value to the outfit would be cut down quite a mite."

Higborn nodded his appreciation of the fact.

"What you aim to do?" he asked.

Slade quickly answered with a question of his own.

"You got two holdin' herds all ready to join tomorrow and shove to the shipping pens in town, Cal, one on your north range, and one on your south. Right?"

"That's right," Higborn agreed.

"Figgering as you do, that your beefs have been rustled through the south end of the valley, which herd will you guard careful tonight?"

"The herd on the south range, of course," Higborn replied instantly.

"Right." Slade nodded. "With that herd well guarded and the boys all on the job, nobody could run the north herd past them, either. That way, both herds would be safe. And I've a hunch," he added with meaning, "that some other gents are gonna figger all that out just like I'm tellin' you. I figger they won't be able to resist that big herd of fat beefs worth a heap of *dinero*. While you're keeping your eyes skinned on your south herd, they'll be plumb busy shovin' the other herd down Mexico way, without a chance of having a loop dropped on them."

"But how in blazes . . . ?" Higborn began.

"I'll tell you," Slade interrupted.

Briefly he outlined what he had discovered in the hills.

"Been looking for just some such thing," he explained. "I figgered first off, from the geological formation of this valley, there should be some old waterways through the hills, naturally by way of one of the cañons. Mebbe a million years back, the floor of this valley was considerably higher than it is now, which means that its side cañons sloped out of the valley instead of into it. Water must have run through those cañons to the west and south in those days. Then came a mighty big and sudden sinking and the valley floor dropped to where it is now. Most of the old waterways got closed up since then, but I figgered mebbe one might still be in existence. There is, and by way of that cows have been run out of this valley."

Higborn shook his head unbelievingly.

"How in blazes did you figger it out?" he asked.

"The night I rode into this section, I saw a herd being pushed along mighty fast . . . to the *north*. I figgered at the time it looked funny. Then when Harley Bell rode in with his head busted and told about the wide-looping, I was plumb shore the herd I saw was yours. It was, as I said, headed north. That's what started me thinking of another way out of this valley. Now let's get busy. Have all the boys ride out to the south holding spot before dark. Those hellions will be keeping a sharp watch on what's going on. Then, after it is good and dark, we'll slip the boys away, all except a couple to keep the fires going and make it look like everybody is on the job at the south holding spot. The rest of us will sneak into that cañon and see what happens. I'm willing to bet a hatful of *pesos* that before daylight tomorrow, there won't be any more rustling to worry about in Lost Valley."

"But if the Injuns ain't doin' it, who is?" demanded old Cal as he stood up and buckled on his gun.

"I've got a good notion, but I'm not saying until I'm plumb shore," Slade replied. "We'll know before morning."

Where the cut brush hid the mouth of the cave, the cañon was dark and silent, with a silence broken only by the mournful sighing of the wind in the leaves. Nothing moved amid the shadows.

Then, faint with distance, sounded the wailing bawl of a tired and disgusted steer. The querulous bleats drew nearer, were undertoned by the low rumble of many hoofs. Moving shadows loomed in the starlight. There was a creaking of saddle leather, a jingle of bit irons, as men dismounted and began removing the cut brush.

Suddenly light flickered, burst into a dazzling glare as oil-soaked brush flamed fiercely. The red light beat on the faces of the CH cowboys, standing grim and ready, guns out. It beat on the faces of the amazed rustlers, and on the square head and livid face of Blaine Ollendorf, standing a little to one side of his men, directing the movements.

In the tense hush, Walt Slade's voice rang out, edged with steel: "You're caught settin'! Don't reach! Get your hands up!"

With a yell of fear and fury, Ollendorf went for his gun. Slade shot him before it cleared leather. The man reeled, pitched forward onto his face, writhed over on his back. The cañon rocked and bellowed with a roar of six-shooters.

It was all over in a minute. Caught by surprise, the demoralized wide-loopers didn't have a chance. Almost instantly four of their number were stretched on the ground. The others threw down their guns and howled for mercy.

"Tie 'em up," Slade ordered tersely. He knelt beside the dying Ollendorf, who glared up at him with filming, hate-filled eyes.

"Cursed swine," he hissed through the blood frothing his lips. "So you're cleaning up, per usual."

Slade slowly shook his head, and held before his eyes the gleaming silver star.

"No," he said quietly, "just the *law* cleaning up . . . per usual."

Ollendorf stared, struggled to rise.

"Damn!" he gasped. "A Ranger!"

Blood poured from his mouth. His head fell back, and he was dead.

The CH cowpunchers secured their prisoners, rounded up the recovered herd, and headed for home. Slightly in the rear, Slade rode with old Cal.

"I never would've believed it of Blaine Ollendorf," said Higborn, shaking his head. "How come you to figger him in the first place, Slade?"

"Didn't have much to go on at first," The Hawk admitted. "Just some mud on a boot scraper. Recollect the morning we rode up to his place? Ollendorf took good care to tell us he'd been in bed sleeping all night, and hadn't yet been out of the house. But there was black mud on his boots, and fresh black mud on the scraper. And his eyes had the look of a man who had been up all night and doing a heap of hard riding. I figgered the mud on the scraper must have come from Ollendorf's boots, and I couldn't help but wonder where he'd picked it up. Mostly red soil hereabouts, you know. And why should he lie about being out during the night? Looked funny. Then, when that hellion dry-gulched you and me by the slope, I did some hard thinking. Ollendorf was the only person we'd spoken to all morning, the only person so far as I could see who knew we were heading for town.

"You'll recollect the trail makes a wide arc from his place, curving west until it reaches the west slope. Straight across Ollendorf's range would be a heap shorter than around the curve. A jigger slipping away from Ollendorf's ranch house as soon as we were out of sight over the bulge could easy make it to the slope ahead of us, hole up, and wait until we came along. Which, I figger, is just what happened. I caught a funny look in Ollendorf's eyes when he first saw me, a surprised look. I figgered right off he'd recognized me as El Halcón. That was OK, but why should he be so anxious to put me out of the way in a hurry?"

"Because, knowin' about you and your reputation, he figgered you were to bust up his game," old Cal shrewdly deduced.

"Right," Slade agreed.

"But why did the hellion take up for the Injuns all the time? Looks like he would've wanted to help make folks suspicious of them."

The Hawk shook his head.

"Was smarter the other way. The natural thing for a guilty jigger was to cast suspicion on somebody else. Ollendorf did the opposite, which really helped put him in the clear. I figger, though, that if things had showed up that proved Mukwarrah and his bucks couldn't be guilty, he would have managed in some way to get folks to looking sideways at Thankful Yates, who's sorta under a cloud."

"Why did you figger first off the Injuns didn't have anythin' to do with it?"

"First off, because of that drum beating you fellers made so much of." Slade chuckled. "That was just another of Ollendorf's tricks. Cal, I know somethin' about Indian customs. About the only time they do any drum beating is when they are having a shindig, or when they're starting on the war-path. Indians are just like the rest of us. If they have any skull-duggery in mind, they don't go advertising it. I reckon you're like most folks who live next door to Indians, you never take the trouble to find out anything about them or their customs."

"I'm goin' to," old Cal declared emphatically. "Come to-morrow, I'm ridin' down to Mukwarrah's place to eat crow. Reckon I plumb owe him a apology."

"Reckon you do," Slade agreed. "And I've a notion you'll get along prime with him. He's a fine old gent."

"What about that Injun who dry-gulched us? And we got three more of the same sort ridin' ahead there with their hands roped."

"That dry-gulchin' gent was an Apache 'breed, with his share of white blood, which mebbe is what made him so ornery," Slade replied.

"How'd you know that?"

"Didn't have the look of a Yaqui, like you said Mukwarrah's tribe was. He'd cut his hair Yaqui style, but when he fell there with his head hanging over, there was a plain sign of a part on the left side. No Yaqui ever parts his hair. I knew right then he couldn't belong to Mukwarrah's outfit, which tied up with what I was already thinking. Ollendorf slipped in a few 'breeds to ride with his wide-loopers, so if anybody happened to get a look at the outfit op-erating, they'd figger first off it was Mukwarrah's Indians."

"Wonder why they tried to hang old Mukwarrah, like you told me about?"

"Part of the scheme to set outfits against each other. That's an old owlhoot trick, and it usually works. Get a coupla outfits on the prod against each other, and *pronto* they blame each other for any skullduggery what's going on.

Which makes it pie for the owlhoots. That's why they set your ranch house afire, though that was possibly done, too, to distract attention from the wide-looping the same night. That herd was sorta close to the ranch house when it was shoved off, wasn't it?"

"That's right. You figger Ollendorf was responsible for Baldy Yates's dry-gulchin'?"

"Wouldn't be surprised. Mebbe Yates might have been smart enough to fenagle old Mukwarrah's land away from him. Ollendorf wouldn't want that to happen, of course. Well, I reckon that's about all. Wanna be gone in the morning before the sheriff comes out rarin' about folks who take the law in their own hands."

Old Cal gazed across the moonlit prairie, and smiled complacently.

"Yeah, it's a plumb pretty range," he said. "A fine place to live, with good neighbors livin' all around you. But I'll be almighty sorry to see you ride off, son."

"Cap Jim's got another mite of a chore ready for me by now," Slade replied. "Mustn't keep him waiting."

He rode away the following morning, tall and graceful atop his black horse. He had uncased his guitar, and back to old Cal came the merry tinkle of the strings, and the music of a rich, sweet voice singing:

> **Oh, there ain't no gals like Texas gals,**
> **That's what I'm here to say,**
> **With their faces golden-freckled by the sun;**
> **So I'm headin' back for Texas,**
> **Yes, I'm headin' back today,**
> **And, boys, I'm glad my shippin' chore is done.**

The Lone Star Peril

I

The harvest moon swept across the arc of the sky and sank in the west. Where its soft glow had been, new stars came winking into sight, and the stars already there shone with a greater brightness. Then secretly, steadily, the earth kept turning, turning, bringing day nearer.

Slowly the sky in the east lightened; reluctantly the stars flickered back before the onward march of the sun. One lonely star, called by men the morning star, lingered. It looked down on the land of Texas—whose sons had taken it for their emblem.

Growing dim before the light from the east, it saw the peaks, the plains and the rivers, the sleeping towns of the white men and the slumbering Indian villages, the herds of cattle asleep or grazing, the wolves skulking the sheep ranges, the coyotes pointing their noses to the sky, the mountain lions hunched by the water holes, the sentinel stallions guarding the wild descendents of the Spanish steeds of the blood-letting *conquistadores*. With the rising sun the morning faded. Then came the mild morning sunshine with its soft breeze blowing out of the west. Peace hung over the wasteland. Here and there life was awakening and beginning to stir.

In the north dust was rising. Once such dust was pounded into the blue air by herds of buffalo, but today it was made by the buffalo's successor, the Texas longhorn. 10,000 of them were moving south—a great clean herd, fresh from a night's rest, driven on by easy stages so as not to melt their fat. For half a mile, from front to rear, the sea of cattle extended and held to orderly formation by the riders on its flanks, while behind rolled the chuck wagon and ahead rode two horsemen, one mounted on a sorrel, the other on a gray.

The man on the gray was elderly but hale. His square-hewn face radiated honesty and strength. Well might men say of John Holcomb that his word was as good as his bond, and that he would live to be 100. The cattle behind him had come from his great spread in the Panhandle.

Hitherto he had always driven his stock to the cattle depots in the north, to Dodge City, Wichita, Winfield, but the old markets were glutted, and new markets had had to be found. John Holcomb, pioneer of the Panhandle, had found one, or rather the new market had found him. That was why, for the first time in Texas history, a trail drive was headed south.

John Holcomb's companion was young, at least thirty years the cattle king's junior. Yet his lean, bronzed face bore a stamp of authority no less powerful than the older man's although its source was neither age nor wealth.

"Yonder's the gap," he was saying, and, as he pointed southward, something flashed on his breast where the sunlight struck it. It was the badge of the Texas Rangers, the silver star in the silver circle. "Nature's cut, made by a long-dead river between the Corazones Mountains an' the Chisos. In an hour's time we'll be in Devil's Pass."

John Holcomb drew a deep satisfied breath. "End o' the trail," he said. "Here's hopin' *Don* Alvarez is already there, waitin' fer us. Then we kin git through our business an' start right back. I'm a mite homesick. Ever been homesick, Markham?"

"Got no kinfolk to be pinin' for," the Ranger answered. "Injuns took 'em when I was a shaver. Reckon the only home

I got is my station, an' the only kinfolks 're my feller Rangers."

"You got a better family than most, then. It shore does beat all how you Rangers do your jobs. No frills, no unnecessary gab. You just go ahead an' do 'em. I'm a heap indebted to you fer steerin' this trail drive."

"All in the day's work. Mebbe you'd better save your thanks until the return trip is finished. When we get into Devil's Pass an' you swap your cows fer the *don*'s silver, the job'll be only half done. I'd feel a damn' sight more comfortable travelin' with a passel o' cows than I'm goin' to feel travelin' back with burros laden down with shinin' bars."

"What makes you say that? Do you reckon there'll be any danger on the return trip?"

"Speakin' in particular, no . . . speakin' in general, yes. Meanin' that wherever there's money there are folks likely to be after it like buzzards after carrion. That's why I ain't never hankered to be rich. There's three things which, so long as I've got 'em on me, I don't pine fer additional wealth. Two of 'ems here"—he tapped his two guns—"an' the third is here." Markham's hand went up to his badge. "I'd grieve mighty sore to lose any one o' them. But so long as I've got all three, I kin reckon myself as rich as John Holcomb, who, in about another hour, will be swappin' a passel o' beef fer two hundred thousand dollars in Mexican silver."

The Ranger accompanied this bit of philosophy with a laugh in which John Holcomb joined.

"Reckon mebbe you're right," Holcolm said. "Mebbe I'd swap all that silver to be young again, like you."

"You ain't got the silver yet," the Ranger said.

Was it a premonition of coming disaster or merely the answer of John Holcomb's aging bones to the mountain breeze that sent a tremor up and down his spine? A cloud had passed across the sun and had momentarily shut away its warmth and light. Was it an omen?

Don José Alvarez waited in Devil's Pass. With his eighty *vaqueros* and his burros laden down with silver, he waited for the coming of the *Americanos*. Already from a distance he heard the thunder of their cattle, and his thin aristocratic face showed his gladness. On and on came that sound, and at last the trail drive, one of the largest that had ever taken place in Texas, came sweeping into the pass.

Don José raised his richly ornamented sombrero. A cheer broke from the throats of his *vaqueros*. It was answered by the whoops of the Texans. The cowpunchers sent the huge herd into a mill, for it would have been impossible to check them in any other way. The thunder of their hoofs echoed and reëchoed from the cañon walls and dust clouds rose, making them misty.

Gradually the cattle were separated into several milling herds. Their pace began to slacken. Soon, under the skillful riding of the cowpunchers, they were under control, peacefully cropping the grass.

Devil's Pass was about a quarter of a mile across from wall to wall. It was as though the prairie had reached a finger into the mountains and left it there to point the way to Mexico. As a place for the actual transfer of the ownership of cattle it was ideal.

John Holcomb and Ned Markham thundered up to the Mexicans. *Don* José held out his hand. John Holcomb grasped it. The handclasp was the symbol of the peace that had come at last after the Texan fight for independence.

"John Holcomb," *Don* José began in slow measured English, "men of our kind do not need papers and lawyers in a transaction of this kind, great as it is. You brought me your cattle. I brought you my silver. Let us exchange them without more ado. We are both far from home and time is precious for both of us. Once more the grass grows in my country and waits but for cattle to graze upon it as in the past, before the drought came. I give you the silver ungrudgingly. I believe you give me your cattle in the same way."

"I do," answered John Holcomb. "I'm powerful glad to be a party to a deal in which both sides get what they want an' nobody loses. As you say, we don't need to sign no papers. The cattle are yours."

"And the silver is yours!"

"An' here's hopin' we meet again to do the same."

Both men raised their hands in signal for the exchange to be made. The *vaqueros*, with great laughing shouts, rode forward. They made no secret of how glad they were to be free of burros and driving cattle again. The Texans, grinning at the tame prospect of driving burros, waited until the Mexicans took over. It was plain that the men from over the Río Grande knew their jobs.

So, in less than half an hour after the two parties had come together, they began to separate, the Texans headed north, the Mexicans headed south. Silver moving to the north, cattle moving to the south, men moving to their homes, Ranger Markham moving to the only home he knew, his station, John Holcomb rich in silver and wishing in vain that he could exchange it, all of it, for Markham's youth, *Don* José thinking of his people and how he could best serve them in the years to come. Texans and Mexicans, formerly enemies, but now....

II

High up on the cañon wall Ranger Markham saw something glitter. It was like the flash of sunlight on steel. Even as his heart leaped in his chest, and his brain sparked a warning, his hand instinctively reacted and plunged for his rifle. He was too late. Two shots came, one following so quickly upon the other that both seemed to sound together.

John Holcomb gazed aghast as he saw the Ranger reel in his saddle, and heard him give a sharp staccato cough. He saw blood spurt from Markham's back, saw him slide from his mount to the ground. But, alas, John Holcomb had not seen what the Ranger had seen. He had seen no glint of sunlight on steel high up on the cañon wall. He thought the shot had come from the Mexicans and his heart flamed up within him. Treachery. Black, unspeakable treachery. John Holcomb's guns were out and his voice was roaring:

"Spread out! Spread out and come in shooting! They've got the cattle an' now they're aimin' to take back the silver!"

The fateful words plunged like daggers into the hearts of the Texans, who had already turned. The face of every one of them was contorted with the impulse to kill, with unimaginable bitterness and anger. The Mexicans—the Mexicans who they had trusted, with whom they had exchanged cigarettes— had played them false, had never meant to let them have the silver, had meant all along to take back the silver after they had given it.

Don José Alvarez did not hear John Holcomb's frenzied

words. He and his party were too far away and the breeze blew in the other direction. But *Don* José had seen one of his *vaqueros* knocked clear out of his saddle and land stone dead upon the ground. Into *Don* José's mind had flashed a thought similar to John Holcomb's. Treachery. *Gringo* treachery. The Texans, now that they had got the silver, meant to take back the cattle. *Don* José, too, had seen no flash of sunlight on steel high up on the cañon wall.

Only the devil could have arranged what was to follow. Texans and Mexicans again at war. Each believing that they had been attacked by the other. Each driven to the pitch of madness by that thought. Treachery. *Gringo* treachery. Greaser treachery! Only to be avenged, washed out, by each other's blood.

In less than a minute, in that first furious charge of cowpunchers and *vaqueros* upon each other, thirteen dead lay on the ground, six Texans and seven Mexicans. The screams of wounded horses rent the air, drowning out the human curses. But John Holcomb was still unhit.

"Take cover!" roared the cattleman. "Take cover to reload!"

They obeyed. They took cover behind dead horses, and those who took cover behind horses that were only wounded mercifully finished off the animals with precious bullets that should have taken human toll. Behind knolls, hillocks, occasional rocks, they took up positions, reloaded, bound up their wounds as best they could. There was no thought of retreat on either side. Nothing but ultimate vengeance could satisfy them, death to the last man of the enemy.

Ranger Markham, the one man who could have told them that what they were doing was wrong, that the whole thing was a horrible mistake, where was he? Dead? No, not dead, but dying. But even then he tried to do his job. His jaws moved; he was saying something. He thought he was shouting, but his words were really coming in whispers. His eyes were filmed, and his voice thickened as the words tumbled from his lips.

"Holcomb . . . *Don* José . . . stop it! For God's sake, stop it! I saw the shot came from the cañon wall. Someone's up there . . . he's sent you flying at each other's throats . . . he's made you think you attacked each other."

The Ranger's nerveless fingers strove to grasp the butts of his six-guns. His eyes rolled upward until the whites showed in his attempt to seek the place in the cañon wall where that first warning glint of sunlight on steel had flashed its message to him in vain.

"By all the honored bones o' dead Rangers," he prayed, and now his voice was not even a whisper but only a movement of the lips from which no sound came forth, "stop this sheddin' of blood. Buck. . . ."

Through the haze of waning consciousness, of oncoming death, he saw his horse's head bending down toward him. "Git goin', Buck." His lips formed the words but no sound came. "Git away from here, far away, else you'll die like your rider that was a part o' you, an' you a part o' him. Git goin'."

But the horse nuzzled him, as though wanting to make him rise and mount again. "Good ol' Buck." The lips barely moved now and Ned Markham's eyes were closing. "In all Texas there wasn't but one hoss that was the beat o' you. Somewhere an *hombre* is a-ridin' him. Wisht Jim was here now, he'd know what to do . . . he always does. He'd know how to stop it. It's gittin' dark . . . I reckon I'm. . . ."

The cañon was filled with gunsmoke but the pungent aroma of it no longer registered on Ned Markham's consciousness. Six-guns crashed ahead, behind, and all around him, but to him the sound was now like the crackle of sticks in a line rider's lonely campfire at night. It had grown dark, very dark, for Ranger Markham.

Just before he died, his right hand strayed away from his six-gun and came to rest upon his Ranger's badge. Blood trickled out from under it. The death-dealing bullet had entered Ned Markham's back, had gone through his body, but had stopped with its nose against the back of the metal emblem.

It was as though the invisible forces of evil, represented by that leaden pellet, had hesitated before the bit of metal that represented the forces of good. Was this, too, an omen? Perhaps the last thing of which Ned Markham was aware before he passed on to ride another and greener range was his badge, wet with blood but still there. And if he had been able to speak to John Holcomb in that moment he would have said: "I'm dyin' rich."

Buck, sniffing death, suddenly threw up his head and let out a heart-stricken whinny. That same instant a bullet found him. The light in his brain went out and he tumbled down to rest beside the master he had outlived by a scant few minutes.

All around the dead Ranger the battle of extermination raged. Men fought in the way they were fighting only when they believed their cause was just. Thus, a Texan and a Mexican, their hot guns empty, their cartridge belts empty, deserted their covers from which they had singled each other out, and fell upon each other like wild beasts. Their Bowies went deep and they sank down together in an embrace that caused their blood to mingle in a common pool.

The one big battle had ended after the first furious charge. From then on it had become a series of individual battles, of man against man. Texan sought out Mexican, Mexican sought out Texan, and from whatever cover they had strove to translate quivering life into stiff death.

A Texan, his Bowie lost, his guns empty, broke from cover and charged forward with a hate-crazed shout. A bullet struck him but he came on. He leaped the rock behind which his enemy crouched, two bodies mingled, and, as a bullet tore up into the Texan's throat, he sent his gun barrel downward with a sickening crash upon the Mexican's head.

So another two men, who should have lived on, who had never intended to do each other any harm, died together. Texan blood bathed the split skull but could not bring life back to the shattered brain.

The gunshots began to come less frequently, the spurts of flame diminished. For the number of duels was decreasing, the participants in them were dying, some by bullet, some by knife, some by the power of bare hands increased tenfold by the lust for vengeance. The end was coming, an end without victory for either side, an end in death that played no favorites.

John Holcomb, a bullet in his shoulder, a bullet in his thigh, his nose broken from a fall he had taken and his face smeared with drying blood, crawled furtively along behind a hillock. No one back in the Panhandle would have recognized him as the man who folks said would live to be 100. For John Holcomb was already 100 years old in spirit. He had aged forty years in as many minutes.

He was old—old and broken—and he did not want to grow any older; he wanted to die. For he saw that life after this, after the death of men who had been like sons to him, would no longer be worth living.

But before he died, he wanted one thing. So he crawled along like an old mountain lion, searching, seeking, looking for something. John Holcomb was looking for *Don* José Alvarez.

And *Don* José? He, too, was looking for something and

that something was John Holcomb. Both men, the cattle king of the Panhandle and the *hidalgo* of Coahuila, were looking for each other, with only one thought in mind—to kill the other, and then to die. For to *Don* José, also, life was no longer worth living. Only a minute before he had crawled away from the dead body of his only son and he knew he could never go back to face his mother.

John Holcomb and *Don* José, looking for each other, found each other. Fate seemed to bring them together. *Don* José came crawling around the hillock. Had he been a bloodhound he could not have smelled out his quarry more unerringly.

As he crawled, the mark of death was already written on his face, and the bloody silk handkerchief that he held with one hand against his chest was additional evidence that his wound was mortal. In the other hand he clutched a knife with a silver handle. Silver. The metal had proved a curse.

His dark eyes flashed into flame as he saw John Holcomb. About ten feet separated them. John Holcomb raised himself on one elbow, the elbow of the hand that held his gun. With a curse on his lips he triggered. There was a *click,* but no sound of a shot—the gun was empty. John Holcomb let it fall. His lips curled away from his teeth as he raised himself to his knees so as to get at his Bowie.

Don José kept crawling toward him slowly, slowly. From his lips, too, curses were coming, low hot curses that called down the wrath of heaven upon the Texan's gray head. And now John Holcomb, the Bowie in his hand, began to move once more. The ten feet that had separated them became five, then three. Meanwhile the life blood kept oozing out of them. And now they were close enough to each other so that, if they lifted their knives, they could bring them down to find a home in each other's flesh.

At that moment the cloud that had hidden the sun moved away. The sunlight glinted on the upraised knives. But the effort to strike was too much for their failing strength. They fell forward, lay prone, and pantingly looked into each other's eyes, only a few inches away.

"*Madre de Dios*, forgive me," *Don* José whispered to himself hoarsely in Spanish. "I have not the strength to execute justice upon this wretch who was not content with an honest bargain. *Madre de Dios*, strike him dead, for I cannot . . . I am too weak . . . I am dying."

John Holcomb understood Spanish. The words entered his ears, and seeped into his consciousness like sounds from a great distance. For an instant they were meaningless to him. Then, as their significance began to penetrate his brain, there spread across his face an expression of horrified disbelief. *Don* José had called *him* a wretch, had accused *him* of not being satisfied with an honest bargain. Bargain? What bargain?

The exchange of cattle for silver had been honest enough. But *Don* José had accused him, John Holcomb, of not being satisfied with it. What did *Don* José mean? That he, John Holcomb, had wanted the cattle, too? But how could that be, when it was *Don* José—not John Holcomb but *Don* José—who had not been satisfied with it? When it had been *Don* José who, not satisfied with 10,000 head of cattle, had perpetrated this diabolical massacre in order to take back the silver? But *Don* José had cursed him, *him*, for what had happened.

"Alvarez," John Holcomb panted, and his eyes were twin pools of agony, "do you think I was after the cattle? Did I hear you straight? Tell me, fer God's sake!"

Into the face of the *hidalgo* there now came the same expression as John Holcomb had worn when the words of the Mexican had reached his understanding—an expression of gathering horror, of aghast disbelief.

"*Sí,*" he answered, his Adam's apple jerking convulsively. "For what, then, dog of a *gringo,* cursed to an eternity in hell, for what you have done!"

"But it was you, *you,*" John Holcomb choked. "You attacked us. You were after the silver. . . ."

"My God, what are you saying? I was after no silver. I was satisfied with the bargain. But you . . . you wanted the silver and cattle both."

"No!" John Holcomb's clenched fist beat weakly on the ground. "No, I tell you! No!"

"Then who . . . who fired the shot that killed . . . that killed my son?"

The awful suspicion of the truth was beginning to come home to both wretched men.

"Who fired the shot into Ranger Markham's back?" John Holcomb mumbled. "My God, what's happened here?"

They looked at each other, horror in their eyes, horror that had its source in the dawning realization that the truth was different than they had thought. They now knew that some incredible deviltry had touched off the spark responsible for the tragedy in Devil's Pass.

"Listen," John Holcomb suddenly whispered.

Sounds that had been coming from both ends of the pass, which had escaped the notice of the dying men up to then, now began to impinge upon their consciousness.

"Listen," John Holcomb said again. Dying as he was, to his ears those sounds brought an unmistakable message. "That's . . . that's cattle bein' rounded up. *Your* cattle. . . ."

Don José turned his head with an agonized effort. "And *your* silver," he muttered. "Sink down. Don't move."

The hillock blocked their view of the cattle roundup that was taking place beyond the southern entrance to the pass, but beyond the northern end, through the smoke and dust, they saw men riding the burros down and bunching them. The shouts grew louder. The burros were being driven into the pass.

The animals balked. They smelled death and were frightened by it, but long cruel whips flashed out. On and on the animals came. John Holcomb and *Don* José lay frozen, feigning death. The drive swept past them, amid shouts and curses.

"They are the murderers," *Don* José murmured brokenly. "Not you, not me. What have we done? Fools and wretches that we are. We have shed each other's blood in a great mistake. Death comes too slow for me. A minute longer of life would be too much agony after what has happened. *Mi amigo,* forgive . . . forgive . . . forgive me."

And *Don* José, groping for his knife, found it. Painfully he raised himself, pointed the knife inward upon himself, and prepared to cast himself down upon it.

"Stop!" John Holcomb said fiercely, with the strength remaining to him. "Forgive? I forgive. Forgive *me.* But that's not the way. I see it all now. We've got to think of the livin'. We're the only ones left alive and that won't be fer long, but while we're livin' we've got to think what to do so that folks will know how an' why we died. Otherwise, they'll think one or the other of us was a hound o' hell. They'll never know the truth."

Don José let the knife fall. Tears rolled down his cheeks. "*Sí, sí,*" he murmured. "It is true. We must leave a record. *Sí.*"

He slipped out of his soiled but richly embroidered jacket. He stripped off his white shirt. With each movement he made a groan escaped him. He spread out the shirt. He picked up the knife again. The wound in his chest had stopped bleeding. John Holcomb saw him look down at it and shake his head. "I reckon I'm still bleedin'," John Holcomb said. "You kin use my blood."

But *Don* José slit the tip of the middle finger of his left hand, and, as the blood streamed out, he dipped the tip of his knife in it and began to write. Carefully, slowly *Don* José wrote their dying testimony. In very small letters, and with as delicate a touch as his failing strength could command, so the blood would not blot, he wrote the following message:

John Holcomb had cattle. José Alvarez had silver. Cattle and silver were exchanged. Then some evil power unknown to us attacked us. Each believed the other guilty but we were wrong. We are dying, but we leave this record, hoping that it will get into the possession of someone, so that our deaths may be avenged.

John Holcomb took the dripping knife that *Don* José held out to him. By a miracle of effort he held his hand steady while he signed. Then *Don* José signed and let fall the knife. They straightened to their knees. Their hands met, clasped, then John Holcomb's eyeballs shot up, his mouth dropped open, and he slumped. *Don* José slumped with him. Both men died together, but they did not let go each other's hands.

They slept their last long sleep and they did not hear the crackle of prairie grass to the north and the south. They did not know that fires had been kindled at both entrances to the pass, fires that were intended to conceal the evil that had been done. Had they written their record in vain? Would the fire consume it, as it would consume them, and would the tragedy of Devil's Pass remain forever an unanswerable mystery, a puzzle of blackened bones, six-guns, knives, which no man could ever solve?

III

In the jumble of hills back of Devil's Pass a man was riding fast. He rode a horse that was a flash of golden flame. At first glance his riding might have been thought reckless and his treatment of his horse cruel, for the terrain was not adapted to such speed. It seemed especially made to break the legs of horses and the necks of their riders.

However, this man and his horse seemed made for each other. Along swales, into gullies, up again, hurtling depressions, they came on together, climbing, always climbing, and eating up the distance between them and the place from which dense smoke was rising.

As Jim Hatfield, from his lathered horse, looked down into Devil's Pass an exclamation broke from him. He threw his glance to the right and left, calculating the speed with which the fires were advancing.

"Goldy," he muttered, "it's too hard from this height to tell whether they're all corpses below or whether some might still be alive. We've got to go down there."

It was characteristic of the Lone Wolf, once his mind was made up, not to hesitate. He started Goldy down the steep descent, and the horse, knowing what was required of him, hesitated no more than did the master. It seemed to Jim Hatfield that the pass came rushing up at him, almost as though he were falling, so quickly did Goldy negotiate the steep and treacherous footing. He was in the pass before he knew it. What he saw caused the blood to leave his face. Death—death everywhere with fire approaching. A horrible shambles that seemed to him to be without rhyme or reason.

"We've got to find out what all this is about an' we ain't got much time," he breathed. "Steady, Goldy . . . don't let the smoke worry you none."

The sun, shining down into the pass, saw a curious sight— a horse and rider dashing now here, now there, looking for life where there was none. Now and then the rider swooped down out of his saddle until his head seemed almost to touch a silent shape on the ground.

"Dead . . . all dead," Jim Hatfield muttered. Then suddenly he cried out, pulled Goldy up short, dismounted, and ran back, Goldy following. Jim Hatfield stood for a moment beside Ned Markham, then quietly removed his broad hat as he stood motionless in the broiling Texas sun.

Jim Hatfield was not a man to show his emotions even when he had time for them. Only the tightening of his jaw revealed his mingled shock and grief. Ned Markham—Ned Markham who had been his bunk mate until transferred to the Carson Ranger station.

"You're gonna git buried, Ned," Hatfield panted, working fast. "This fire ain't gonna git you. God, what a killin!"

He made the body fast across the front of his saddle and continued his rapid inspection without re-mounting. "It's gittin' warm" he muttered. "We'll have to be gittin' out o' here soon."

Hatfield hurried around the hillock behind which two men lay with hands clasped. He looked at their faces; he picked up the shirt, and quickly read its message. A stony, terrible look was in his eyes when he had finished. He mounted. Raising a clenched fist to the sky, his voice expressing his realization of the tragedy that had come upon all these dead men, Mexicans and Texans, he shouted: "Good bye, you-all! I'm sorry I can't take all of you out o' here! One's all I kin take! But I'll be back! I promise, I'll be back! I'll make the responsible varmints pay if it takes my lifetime. I promise!"

The last words came sobbing up out of his throat. Then, his way to the north and south cut off by fire, he rode straight for the cañon wall, not the one that he had descended, which was too far away, but the opposite one. He heard a shot, felt a slug tear into his shoulder, looked up, saw the glint of sunlight on steel. So that was how it had been done. That was the kind of shot described by the message on the shirt.

Trapped! Cut off from the north and the south by fire, cut off from the west by an unseen sharpshooter! He wheeled Goldy and thundered toward the eastern wall. A fusillade of shots came down.

Looks like I'm takin' no one out o' here, he thought grimly. "We've got to go through the fire, Goldy."

Hatfield headed north. And now no restraining hand was on the bridle. Each hand held a six-gun. But Goldy responded to the pressure of the knees on his flanks. Straight for the smoke and flame he galloped, into it, through it for what seemed like an age, and finally burst into the open at the northern end of the pass.

Horse and rider must have seemed like an apparition out of hell to the group of mounted men that blocked the way. Before they could get their weapons into action, Hatfield's guns were roaring. With lighting like speed he triggered, saw men toppling from saddles. So swiftly did he come on, that one mounted figure did not have time to get out of his path. The Ranger sent the barrel of his gun crashing down upon this one's head. Goldy kept going.

The element of surprise gave Hatfield the advantage he needed. Yet he knew that, if he followed a straight course, he could not maintain it. He knew he would be pursued and that

Goldy, carrying double weight, could not maintain the terrific initial pace. But the plain was not level, it rolled and dipped, and a single rider could pass unseen for miles provided he had the skill to calculate time and distance, his own speed, the speed of his pursuers, and match his calculations with the constantly changing nature of the terrain.

With Hatfield it was more instinct than calculation. Even Goldy seemed to sense that his master was engaged in a life and death game of hide-and-seek, and that the object was to make not distance but the rolling plain itself an ally in their escape. So the course was not straight but zigzag, and brought horse and rider after an hour's flight only a mile north of Devil's Pass, but several miles to the west of it.

Here Hatfield slowed Goldy to a walk. A mirthless chuckle escaped him. "That's over," he muttered.

He looked down at the body of Ned Markham and shook his head. He was thinking that if he were free, if the corpse of Ned Markham were not with him, he could go back in the direction of Devil's Pass and find out more about what had happened there. He was thinking of the waste of precious time that his possession of the body entailed. But there was no choice. He remembered the wish the dead man had expressed when alive—to be buried when he died in headquarters ground, with the flag of Texas as his winding sheet.

"All right, boy," Hatfield said softly. "It'll be as you wanted. I'm takin' you back to where you want to be. Git along, Goldy."

And Jim Hatfield set himself for the long ride home. The sun would set and still see him riding. The stars would come out and move across the heavens, looking down on the lonely rider carrying his burden of death. The morning star would see and greet him. And throughout his long journey his fighter's heart would be torn between his duty to the dead

and his impatient desire to be where he knew he ought to be—
back at the scene of the massacre, picking up the trail of the
still unknown men who had sullied God's clean mountains
with unspeakable mass murder.

Burning in his mind were the words that were written in
blood upon a shirt, words that his intuition made him fear
were true, words that *Don* José had written down in death:
**We leave this record, so that our deaths may be
avenged.** Jim Hatfield felt that was only the beginning of
some sinister plan.

The moon, rising that night, saw Hatfield riding north,
but it also saw other things. It saw a party of horsemen cross
the Pecos River five miles above the Comanche reservation.
It saw them ride east through the rich range lands that were a
part of the Great Angela Mesa.

In the past five years, thanks to a generous government,
this corner of the mesa had been taken up by small ranchers.
Individually the holdings were small. Taken together, they
spread out over several counties.

The moonlight shone down on half-naked bodies. Comanches! What were Comanches doing away from their reservation?

The horsemen, previously bunched, spread out in a fan-
like formation. Suddenly each one of them held aloft a lighted
torch, which he flung back behind him. Once more they were
bunched but now they were riding hard. The fires they had
kindled followed them, but their horses were fleet and kept
them well ahead of the flames. They rode in silence, grim,
sinister, savage. Only the pound of hoofs and the soughing
sound of flames scourged along by the cool prairie wind rose
in the night air.

Soon other sounds were heard—the bellow of cattle, the
cries of men. Dark clumps on the prairie transformed them-

selves into blindly plunging, terror-stricken longhorns. Sleepy-eyed men rose up startled from under blankets, dazedly reached for their six-guns on seeing the shadowy shapes of the marauders looming large, and were shot down or tomahawked before they had drawn their holstered weapons. The marauders sped on, but the fire took their place, and the waddies who had not been lucky enough to be shot dead knew a few seconds of torment before death finally came to them.

The fire swept on, but the marauders kept ahead of it. A ranch house loomed into sight. A door was flung open; the moonlight etched the figure of a man in the door. He fell with a low moan. There was a high-pitched shriek, which was answered by a mocking yell from the throats of the marauders. A woman knelt by the wounded man. A frightened child clung to her dress. Out of the bunkhouse half a dozen cowboys now erupted.

"Vance!" the woman screamed, and the men came running. "Vance," the woman addressed the spread's top hand, "Phil's wounded. We've got to get him into town to a doctor."

"Ma'am," Vance said, "we've all got to get out o' here. The prairie's on fire. I'll hitch up the buckboard an' drive you two an' the little feller in. The boys kin take keer o' themselves."

The woman cried aloud in despair. "The spread, Vance! What will become of the spread?"

"Can't stop. We've got to get out o' here. Far as I kin see, the Bar X is doomed. That fire's gonna burn clear down to Russel's Ford. Come on, ma'am. It cuts me to the heart, but I can't let you go back into the house fer anything. There's no time. Look, the boys have got the buckboard waitin' already."

Under his insistence the woman obeyed. "The boys will try to save what they can," was Vance's consoling comment as the buckboard got under way.

Tears rolled down the woman's cheeks. "We were happy here," she said. "The spread was paying."

Then she tightened her lips. She was of pioneer stock. No use crying over spilt milk. The grass would grow again. They would come back in a year and start to rebuild—if her husband lived.

They were not the only ones burned out that night. The county seat of Morrow received the refugees from six small ranches. Lights burned in every house. Men congregated on the streets and in the saloons. No one went to bed in Morrow that night, and feelings ran high. Nash Saurel, foreman of the great Maxwell spread, hit the nail on the head, from the cowmen's point of view.

"It's what comes o' parleyin' with Injuns instead o' clearin' them out o' Texas," Saurel told them. "The folks in Washington are too far away to know what it's all about. They give the Rangers authority to deal with the Comanches an' what happens? They make a treaty with Mornin' Star, the big chief, who swears by the Great Spirit that he wants peace. In exchange fer the promise o' peace, the Rangers give Mornin' Star a deed that doubles the size o' the reservation. I tell you, if you give a Injun an inch, he'll take a foot. Raidin's in their blood. It won't be stopped by treaties. It'll only be stopped by lead. The only good Injun's a dead 'un, an' I'm thinkin' it's time we made every damned Injun a good Injun."

What would Jim Hatfield have said if he had heard that? Jim Hatfield had been the man who had negotiated that treaty with Morning Star, the Comanche chief. It was from the reservation that Jim Hatfield was returning, when his homeward journey was interrupted by the black business in Devil's Pass.

To him had been entrusted the delicate mission, because he not only understood the Indian tongue, but Indian psychology as well. What would he have said on hearing that the Comanches were on the warpath again, that they had broken the treaty scarcely forty-eight hours after Morning Star had placed his ratifying mark upon it?

But Jim Hatfield was miles away, nearing headquarters, at the time Nash Saurel of the Maxwell Ranch was making his declaration. He was riding to his station, to report the success of his treaty-making mission and to inform Captain McDowell of the tragic things he had seen in the inferno so well-named Devil's Pass.

IV

Although it was only five o'clock in the morning, Captain McDowell was already at his desk when Jim Hatfield, haggard-faced and weary from lack of food, entered his office. The light of welcome leaped in the grim old soldier's eyes but just as quickly faded—it was as though he had purposely suppressed it.

"Shut up," he said, although Hatfield had not yet opened his mouth. The stern old man went to the door, flung it open, and shouted: "Hot grub an' a pot o' coffee! *Pronto!*"

The food was brought. Hatfield ate ravenously. When he had finished, the captain said: "Anyone could see you hadn't et fer quite a spell."

Hatfield looked at him. "An' anyone kin see that somethin's eatin' you. I reckon it's the first time I ever come back from a job to be greeted with a . . . 'Shut up.' . . . from my cap'n. I don't half like it."

"Then lump it," said the captain bluntly. "I ain't pleased with you, Jim Hatfield. You were sent to make peace with Morning Star. Did you do it?"

For answer Hatfield drew a document out from under his shirt and threw it on the desk. He, too, was growing angry. The captain scanned the paper, folded it, and threw it back at him.

"That ain't peace," he said. "That's a piece of paper. A telegram was relayed from Carson to this station early this morning. The Comanches are on the warpath! What have you got to say, Jim?"

Hatfield did not show the shock these words gave him. His mind flashed back to the council teepee of the Comanches. Again he saw Morning Star making his mark. Again he clasped the Indian's hand.

" 'Tain't so," Hatfield said bluntly.

"Then you've got a strange notion o' peace. Six spreads destroyed by fire, a dozen men killed, one woman. An' Jim Hatfield, instead o' bein' on the scene, is here, talkin' to me. . . ."

"You don't give me much chance to talk, Cap'n," Hatfield interrupted, his eyes hard, but pain at the harsh words of the captain back of them. "Yes, I'm here, an' you're right when you say I should be elsewhere, but not where you think. Ned Markham, from Carson Ranger station, came back with me, Cap'n."

"What's that got to do with it? Where is he?"

"Waitin' outside. I'll bring him in."

Stony-faced, Hatfield went out, and came back bearing the body of Ned Markham. "Here he is, Cap'n," he said.

Captain McDowell swallowed hard. Folks said that the reason the captain looked even older than his years was that the death of a Ranger added a year to his age. His eyes blinked rapidly.

"Talk, Jim," he said without looking at the Lone Wolf.

Tersely but vividly Hatfield told what he had seen in Devil's Pass. The captain read the message written in blood upon the shirt. Then he looked at the body of Ned Markham. His eyes were sad.

"The ways o' chance are strange," he said. "It might've been you instead o' Ned. You didn't know that, did you? The Rangers were asked fer their best man to guide the Holcomb trail drive south, but you were away, makin' peace with the Comanches. So Ned was chosen. An' now he's dead. An' the peace you were supposed to make turns out to be war."

"The peace that I was supposed to make I made," Hatfield said, his voice low. "I'd stake my life that it still stands. I'd stake more than my life. I'd stake my commission in the Rangers. When Morning Star took my hand, I looked into his heart. You tell me the Comanches are on the warpath. I don't believe it. I've got nothing but a hunch to go on, but that hunch is that the massacre in Devil's Pass and these Indian raids tie in together. Things like that don't happen one after the other without some meaning that we can't yet see. Where did these raids happen?"

"Across the Pecos in the southwestern corner of the Great Angela Mesa."

"All right," Hatfield answered, his eyes drawn to pinpoints of determination. "I'll go back there."

Captain McDowell nodded. No suggestion came from him that Hatfield should head a troop instead of going alone. Time had long since proven the wisdom of a remark once made by the taciturn Lieutenant Carney, who upon the occasion of Hatfield's transfer to Bill McDowell's troop, had said: "When he's with a troop, he's just another good Ranger, but when he's off alone, he's a terror. A lone wolf, that's what he is."

The name had stuck.

"I'm sorry I can't stay fer Ned's burial," Hatfield said, "but I reckon he'll understand."

He knelt beside the body, but not to say farewell. He was not ready for that yet. There were things he still might learn before he left the station. He unpinned the dead ranger's badge and passed it up, clotted with blood, to Captain McDowell. An exclamation escaped him and his Bowie knife came out. With it he extracted the bullet that had caused the Ranger's death. He looked at it.

"Ever see anything like this before, Cap'n?"

Captain McDowell took the bullet and examined it. "Rifle bullet," he said, "but longer an' heavier than any I've ever met up with."

Hatfield agreed. "Came down at an angle an' from considerable distance. Otherwise, it would have smashed the badge an' come out." He reached into his pocket. "Here's what looks like a mate to it."

"Where'd that come from?" asked McDowell eagerly.

"I took it out o' my own hide."

Hatfield put the bullets back in his pocket. "Mebbe if I find the gun that fired those shots, I'll find the *hombre* who pulled the trigger. Then we'll be gettin' somewhere. Well, my stomach is full, an' I reckon Goldy is sufficiently rested to carry me to where I want to go. Good bye, Cap'n."

The sun climbed up the heavens and set. The moon and the stars came out. It was dawn before Jim Hatfield reached the Comanche reservation. The Lone Wolf approached it with his left hand on Goldy's bridle, his right hand raised palm outward, in token that he came in peace. While still a good distance off, he had seen two sentinel horsemen, each on one of the low hills that formed a natural entrance to the reservation, drawing a bead on him with their rifles. When he had come near enough to be recognized, they lowered their weapons and waited.

"I have come back," the Ranger said simply in their own tongue. "The message that sings over the wire, that enables the white men to talk together over long distances, sent a tale of trouble ahead of me to my home. Now I find you standing sentinel, as in the bad days of old that I thought were forever gone. Sentinels are not needed where there is peace."

"There is no peace, Lone Wolf," was the answer, "but it is not we Comanches who have broken it. Of all white men, you are the only one who could have approached these hills today without hearing our rifles speak to keep you out. The heart of our chief is full of trouble. He has anxiety for his people, for the whites believe the Comanches have done evil things. And the whites have declared that we are to be driven out of the land."

"Take me to your chief," said Hatfield.

"It is well," was the reply. "You will be a part of the early morning council."

"Of war?" asked the Ranger.

"Of war . . . for defense," the brave replied.

In the central village of the reservation Hatfield found Morning Star addressing a circle of seated figures, each naked to the waist, armed and painted for war. "We will not wait for the whites to come with their torches," the chief was saying. "The palefaces have taught us that the best defense is attack. We will see if what they say is true. . . ." He stopped short on seeing the Ranger. "Why have you come back, Lone Wolf?" he asked sharply.

"To ask a question," Jim Hatfield answered.

"Ask it."

The Ranger dismounted and advanced to the center of the circle. He then stood facing the chief.

"When I last departed from here," he said, "I bore a paper which was the Comanches' promise of peace and the white man's promise to give to the Comanches the virgin land to the north and west of their present reservation. Have the Comanches kept that peace?"

"They have."

"Six ranches have been put to the torch. Twelve white men and one white woman have been killed. Have the Comanches done these things?"

"No."

Hatfield moved closer, until he could see the color of the other's eyes.

"Does Morning Star swear by the Great Spirit that it was not the Comanches who committed those raids?"

"Morning Star swears by the Great Spirit that the word given to the Lone Wolf was not a false word, that the mark he made was not a false mark, that he meant peace when he made it and wants peace now, but that he will defend himself and his people against all attack. The voice of Morning Star is bitter, for his heart is bitter.

"Morning Star's scouts have reported that the whites are preparing to make war against him, that the whites have declared their purpose to be to drive us from our lands, the lands that have been ours and the lands that were to be given us with the coming of the new moon. The whites have invented a name for the man who gives and then takes back . . . Indian giver. The white man does what he accuses us of doing . . . giving and then taking back."

"What evidence has the white man that it was the Comanches who committed arson and murder?" the Ranger asked.

"The white men claim that the trail of the marauders led back to our reservation."

"Is that true?"

"Yes," said Morning Star contemptuously. "The trail led back, but it was not made by Comanches. The golden-haired scalp that was found not far off, and that lay on the prairie as though dropped by accident, was not taken by a Comanche. The white men in Morrow are using it to inflame the whole range against us. On the morning following the raids, we awoke to find strange horses and cattle in our midst. They were animals belonging to the burned ranches, but we did not steal them, and we have driven them out. The ranchers say it was Comanches who burned and killed, but Comanches do not ride horses that wear shoes. And our scouts, who were sent out to the scene of the raids as soon as we learned that we were being accused of them, found tracks of many shod horses. There were a hundred horsemen, they said . . . perhaps more."

"And did they all ride horses that were shod?"

Morning Star seemed to hesitate. "No," he said reluctantly. "About half were shod, the others not."

"Then Indians did take part in the raids."

"White men can ride unshod horses."

Hatfield's mind was busy. "I see that what you are trying to tell me, Morning Star, is that the Comanches are not guilty, but that someone is trying to make it appear that they are."

"I tell you only that the Comanches are not guilty, and you may draw any conclusion you like from that."

The Lone Wolf eyed the chief. "Do you trust me, Morning Star?" he asked earnestly.

Again the chief hesitated before answering. "I no longer know who to trust," he said finally.

Hatfield thought quickly. His mind was made up to one thing—that another Indian war had to be avoided at all costs.

"Your words are harsh, Morning Star, but I am not angered by them. I do not ask you to trust me. I only ask you to listen to me and then to tell me if my words are wise."

"I listen," said Morning Star.

The Lone Wolf's face grew stern and cold. "Why is Morning Star foolish?" he suddenly rapped out. "Why is he preparing to play the game of evil men?"

Morning Star looked at him, puzzled.

"Yes, Morning Star, that is what you are preparing to do," Hatfield went on more softly. "Do you not see it?"

"I do not understand."

"Look. Ranches are burned, palefaces are murdered. Who is guilty? Not the Comanches. But who are accused? The Comanches. Where does the trail of murder lead back to? This reservation. Who made that trail? Not the Comanches. But who wished to make it appear that the Comanches made that trail? We do not know. Let us call him the evil-doer. Why did that evil-doer cause the trail to lead back to this reservation? Because he wanted to make the ranchers believe that the Comanches were the criminals. What did he hope would happen if the ranchers believed that? War. War between white men and red men. What is Morning Star preparing to do? He is preparing to fight. Does not Morning Star see that if he fights, he will be doing what this unknown evil-doer *wants* him to do?"

Morning Star was silent, but only for a moment. "It is true talk," he said. "Your words are words of wisdom, they issue from your mouth like a clear stream of pure water. But what are we to do if your people attack us? Will we have any choice, then, but to fight?"

The theory that had all along been taking shape in Hatfield's mind was growing clearer and clearer. "Does not Morning Star see that this evil-doer, who is attempting to use the Comanches for his own purposes, may also be attempting to use my people for the same purpose? My people are not malicious, Morning Star. If they are inflamed with hate against you and yours, it is only because they have been deceived."

"But what if they attack us," Morning Star persisted, "as my scouts report they are preparing to do?"

"Morning Star, you must *not* fight."

"Is the Lone Wolf mad!" the chief exclaimed with impatience. "Does he expect Comanche braves to stand with folded hands while their homes are burned? To every man the

89

Great Spirit has given the right to defend himself. Does the Lone Wolf want us to give up this right, to stand and take the white men's bullets without giving any in return?"

"The Lone Wolf seeks only to avoid a needless war. What will happen if there is war? Many of my people will be killed, many of your people will be killed. Who will be the gainer? Not my people, not yours. Only the evil-doer."

For a moment there was a deep silence. Then Morning Star spoke. "But how can the war be avoided, if your people attack us? All that the Lone Wolf says is true. But it is not *we* who seek war. It is we who are threatened with attack. And if we are attacked, we must fight. Why does not the Lone Wolf go to his own people and say to them what he has said to us? Why does he not say to them . . . you must not fight. Why does the Lone Wolf say it only to us?"

"Because the Lone Wolf cannot be in two different places at the same time," Jim Hatfield retorted promptly. "The Lone Wolf is not a god. I ask your promise to keep the peace. If you give it to me, I will do my part to prevent any attack on you."

"And if you fail? Will that relieve us of our promise to you?"

"No," said Hatfield thoughtfully. "I will not permit men, be their skins white or red, to be killed in a purposeless war. But I need Morning Star's help. I have thought of a way to avoid bloodshed. It is a hard way, and already I hear Morning Star cry out against it, but it is the only way."

"Speak. Tell us what it is."

"If my people come to attack you," said Hatfield, speaking slowly, "I want them to find waiting for them a wall of Comanche women and children. Yes, I want Comanche braves to hide behind women and children. Stop!"

The murmur of protest from the council ring grew to a

roar. The Lone Wolf raised both his arms for quiet. "Oh, I know that Morning Star is brave!" he cried. "I know that you all, all are brave. Will I think you any less brave if you adopt my plan? No! I will think you even braver, for you will have shown that you are not afraid of being called cowards, and that is the greatest bravery of all. Do this! Prevent war! Give me time to do my work! And I promise you that in the end you will receive the land that was promised to you."

The murmurs of protest still rose, but Morning Star silenced them with a look. "You ask us to do a hard thing," he said softly, "the hardest thing that was ever asked of Comanches, but we will do it. Yes, we will do it." The chief's eyes suddenly flashed. "But woe betide the man who thereafter calls any Comanche a coward for having done so, be he white or red! Him we will not spare, but will kill before the echo of the hateful word has died away. Is it well, Lone Wolf? Are you satisfied now?"

Jim Hatfield's heart swelled. The first battle fought and won. There would be other and harder ones, but the beginning was good.

"It is well, Morning Star," Hatfield said, a bleak smile on his face. "I am satisfied."

In his mind was the memory of the shambles of Devil's Pass, where Texans and Mexicans had annihilated each other in the unknowing service of unknown forces of evil. White ranchers and Comanches had been preparing to do the same thing. More than ever was Hatfield convinced that the events of Devil's Pass were tied in with the Indian raids.

The method of the unknown was the same. The only difference was that the Ranger had arrived at Devil's Pass after the tragedy, whereas he had come to the reservation before a tragedy had taken place. It was an important difference. Nevertheless, Jim had the feeling that he was sitting on a powder mine, that it required only a spark to set the entire range aflame. He was convinced now that an evil force was at work.

The burden of responsibility weighed heavily upon Hatfield's mind. He knew that he was working for the most part in the dark. His mind and heart were restless, as they always were whenever there was any delay in his coming to actual physical grips with the forces behind the scene.

He hastily ate the breakfast provided by Morning Star and set out for Morrow. There, he knew his task would be harder. In accordance with his custom of never showing his hand until he thought the time was ripe, he put his badge in his pocket. He had no definite plan. He knew he would have to depend on his skill in meeting each particular situation as it arose, but he was used to that.

The first situation confronted him sooner than he had expected.

V

It came in the shape of nearly 500 horsemen, galloping toward him across the plain.

"There's my Indian War," he muttered grimly, "the war that's got to be stopped before it starts. Goldy, we've got our work cut out fer us. Trouble aplenty, but we're gonna meet it head-on."

He suited the action to the words, pointing Goldy's head straight for the center of the oncoming troop. With satisfaction he saw that they had noticed his maneuver, for the troop slowed.

"Curious," he murmured, with a low chuckle that contained no mirth. "They want to know who you an' me are, Goldy."

He was right but, being modest, he did not realize how much his own appearance had to do with it.

"Don't look like anyone we know," said the leader of the troop to the man who rode next to him. "He's shore a-comin'. Mebbe he's got some news o' the Comanches, seein' as that's the direction he's headin' away from."

The leader held up his hand in signal for a halt to be made. The troop surveyed the oncoming rider curiously. Hatfield rode up to the leader and waved his hand in greeting to the rest.

"Howdy," he said. "Mighty large gatherin'. Off to a barbecue somewheres, mebbe?"

A raucous laugh came from a man who rode out from the

93

body of the troop and drew up alongside the leader. "Right, stranger. We're off to a barbecue, if you want to call it that. Care to join us?"

The Ranger shook his head regretfully. "Wish I could, but I got no time fer pleasure. I heard tell there was work fer top-hand cowpokes over in the Great Angela Mesa, so here I be. Any o' you gents know of a job I can git?"

The man who had laughed now swore. "Come on, Morgan," he said. "We ain't got no time to waste on tramp cowboys."

"Wait a minute, Saurel," the leader said mildly. He had been studying Hatfield and what he had seen had impressed him. Sam Morgan was a judge of men and he was pretty certain that this stranger was no ordinary cowpoke. He had taken note of the way Hatfield's holsters were slung—low and to the front, and the ends not tied down. That meant that they could be flipped around, leaving the gun butts protruding where the hands could seize and draw without an instant's delay.

"What's your handle, stranger?" he asked.

"Hatfield," the Lone Wolf answered. "Jim Hatfield. I see by the brand on your hoss that your off the Circle Seven spread. Say, there's an outfit I'd like to hitch on to. Folks talk o' the Circle Seven clean down to the border, where I come from."

"I own it," said Sam Morgan, looking pleased. "Hatfield, I like your looks. I reckon I kin give you a job. In fact, the job's yours right now. Do you accept?"

"Why shore, Mister . . . Mister . . . ?"

"Morgan . . . Sam Morgan. You're workin' fer Sam Morgan now, which means, of course, that you're takin his orders."

"Shore thing, boss," the Ranger agreed with feigned eagerness.

"Then my first order is fer you to join this troop, which is on its way to clean the Comanches out o' Texas. Saurel . . ."—he turned to the man on his left—"I know a first-class fightin' man when I see him. You thought I was wastin' time, eh? Well, I've added a valuable recruit to our ranks. Come on, boys. Let's go."

"Jest a minute, Mister Morgan," Hatfield said, his hand raised, and it was strange how effective that mild gesture was in keeping the troop motionless. "Joinin' a cow outfit ain't the same as joinin' the army. You're my boss, but you ain't my commandin' officer. So I reckon I kin ask a few question, which I couldn't do if I was in the army. I'm admirin' your perspicacity in knowin' a first-class fightin' man when you see him. But I can't say I admire a trick that takes advantage of a man's need o' three squares a day an' a bunk."

Sam Morgan flushed to the roots of his iron-gray hair. He was used to authority and unaccustomed to being told off in this quiet, yet effective way. He was the more angry for realizing that the stranger was partially right. But Sam Morgan was not the man to admit himself in the wrong until anger had had time to cool, when, as usually happened, it was too late. "OK, Hatfield," he snapped, "if that's the way you feel about it, you're fired! Come on, boys. Let's get going."

"Not so fast, Mister Morgan!" Hatfield rapped out, and again his raised hand caused the troop to hesitate. *Time,* he thought to himself, *I've got to give Morning Star time, in case I can't stop these* hombres. Aloud he went on: "I didn't say I wasn't *takin'* your orders, Mister Morgan. I said somethin' about *questionin'* 'em. I've fit Injuns in my time, but, when I did, I always knew why I was fightin' 'em. That's what I aim to know now. Why? It can't be that you gents are out after the Comanches fer what they did a year or two ago. What's past is past, an' a couple o' Comanches got hanged fer it.

You don't mean to tell me. . . ."

"We mean to tell you this," Nash Saurel broke in. And he proceeded to describe the recent happenings. "Though why we got to explain things to this cowboy tramp," he ended disgustedly, addressing Sam Morgan, "is more than I kin see."

"That's the story, Hatfield," said Sam Morgan. "Are you joinin' us?"

"No," Jim Hatfield said simply, but so clearly that the word carried to the ears of every member of the troop.

So confident had they all been that the answer would be yes that for an instant there was no response, nothing but an amazed and indignant silence. Then the troop found tongue.

"The low-down varmint's yeller," a stentorian voice burst out.

"Mebbe he's a Injun himself. He looks like one."

"He was comin' from the direction of the reservation. Mebbe he's tied in with 'em."

"Seems to me we ought to take care of him before goin' on . . . with a rope, I mean."

"There must've been a Comanche in his maw's woodpile. . . ."

The Lone Wolf's face had been stony, expressionless, as the quickly mounting passions of the ranchers and their men broke over him, but at this last remark his eyes became suddenly terrible. They bored into the man who had made it—it was Vance Thompson, who had driven Mrs. Judson and her child into Morrow that tragic night.

Hatfield's hands hung loosely down at his sides, but the keen eyes of Sam Morgan noticed how easy it would have been for him to draw and shoot. Vance Thompson wouldn't have stood a chance. Sam Morgan had never before seen a man take an insult like that without attempting to wipe it out in blood. He was puzzled, and more than ever convinced that this stranger was something more than an ordinary cowpoke.

I've hired an' fired an hombre *that's somebody,* he thought. *I'm thinkin' I ought to hire him back again. There's somethin' strange about that* hombre. *He shore put me in my place over that job deal and damned if he wasn't right. Strikes me he's more accustomed to givin' orders than takin' 'em. The way he's lookin' at Vance now, I wouldn't like to have him lookin' at me that way. If looks could kill, Vance Thompson would be dead. Hatfield is keepin' an iron grip on himself. An' Vance . . . Vance looks scared, an' kind o' sorry fer what he said. He feels like me, that this stranger is somebody. The stranger looks like he's about to say somethin' to him. . . .*

Morgan was right. Jim Hatfield was speaking, and speaking directly to Vance. Strangely enough, his voice was gentle and without malice.

"I don't kill without cause," the Ranger was saying, "otherwise, you'd be dead now. I don't look upon what you said as cause fer killin', for I kin see you spoke out of excitement an' ignorance. Consequently I'm forgettin' it. It's forgotten." He turned his eyes on Sam Morgan. "You was sayin' somethin' about some Comanche raids. I kin see you're all wonderin' why I, jest one man, has sort o' got in the way o' five hundred, meanin' you-all. Mebbe 'tain't my business. Mebbe I hadn't ought to butt in this way, an' say no when you-all say yes. But my pappy once told me . . . 'Son,' he sez, 'it's allus a man's business to see that justice is done. But it's also a man's business to see that *injustice* *isn't* done. An' even if it's no skin off his nose whether it's justice or injustice, it's his business jest the same.'

"Now, maybe it ain't no skin off my nose whether you go after the Comanches or not . . . only there's a little somethin' that puzzles me about all this business. Mister Morgan, if I convinced you that if you stopped chawin' tobacco fer one day, I'd give you a thousand dollars the next, an' you knew that was the only way to get the thousand, you'd stop chawin' tobacco, wouldn't you?"

"I'd stop chawin' fer a hull week," Morgan answered. "What are you drivin' at? Keep your shirt on, Saurel. The Comanches'll keep."

"Well," said Hatfield, "it seems to me powerful strange that the Comanches should go on raidin' parties not two days after the government gave 'em written promise to ownership o' more additional land than they got right now. They already got by treaty more than they could ever hope to get by raids . . . land, seed, breed stock. So these raids just don't make sense. Didn't you know about that treaty, Mister Morgan? Notices was posted in all the towns. Didn't any o' you gents know about it?"

There was no immediate answer.

"I see you *did* know about it," said Hatfield, "but I kin also see you had to be reminded about it. If you'll forgive my sayin' so, you-all seem to have let your emotions git the upper hand o' you. If you'd done some thinkin', you might've put two an' two together."

Sam Morgan's face was troubled. It was plain that what Hatfield said impressed him. He looked around to see whether or not his uncertainty was shared by the others. It was. They talked among themselves, and their voices were low and hesitant. But there was one among them who did not hesitate. An oath broke from Nash Saurel. His hand shot up and he was seen to wave something in the air.

"Does this look like the work of anyone but an Injun?" he shouted. "Does it? Does it?"

It was the golden-haired scalp.

"Let's see that," Hatfield said. His voice was low, authoritative.

Nash Saurel hesitated.

"Give it to him," Sam Morgan ordered.

"Mister Morgan," Saurel said, "it beats me why we stand here takin' orders from an alkali tramp we never seed till today. If he hadn't come along, we'd've had the Comanches streakin' to the border by now. Look at it, you-all! It was once on Margaret Kirkland's head! You all knew her, an' a finer woman never lived! An' we stand here in a useless powwow with an interferin' waddy who might be a renegade white man fer all we know, playin' us fer fools while the Comanches have time to prepare fresh deviltries! I don't understand you, Sam Morgan," Saurel went on "but you're leader o' this posse, so I'm takin' your orders. *Here!*"

The last word was addressed to Hatfield, and with it Nash Saurel flung the scalp in his face. The Ranger's hand was a flash of light, and he caught it. Something like a sigh rose from the troop. They all had about the same thought: a man who could react with a speed like that would be deadly with his guns.

Hatfield looked at the scalp. His eyes were sad as he felt the softness of that blonde hair. But in them also was a new glitter. He amazed them by putting the scalp away in his own saddlebag instead of returning it.

"Hey!" Nash Saurel broke out.

"You folks don't seem to know much about Injuns," Hatfield said. He seemed to be talking more to himself than to the troop, but they all heard him. The prairie seemed to have grown very quiet. "This scalp was never taken by a Comanche," he went on. "It was taken by an Apache."

Texas Morgan was standing on the porch of the Circle 7's

picturesque and rambling ranch house, when she saw the
troop approaching. She shaded her eyes with a slim, tanned
hand as she gazed westward unbelievingly.

"It's Father and the boys!" she exclaimed suddenly to the
tall man next to her. "They're coming back. That must
mean that there hasn't been a battle, after all. I'm glad. I
can't tell you how glad I am, Mister Maxwell. I argued and
argued with Father. I kept telling him that even if the Comanches were guilty of those raids, nothing good would ever
come of the ranchers' taking the law in their own hands. The
Indians are wards of the government. It's up to the government to handle them if they get out of control, but Father
wouldn't listen. You know how headstrong he is. I'm sure
that if you'd have been here, the posse would never have
been organized. You're always so cool. You'd have calmed
Father down."

The stern dark-eyed man looked down at her from his
height, taking pleasure in the red lips that sent the words out
in a warm stream, in the color that glowed in the smooth
tanned cheeks.

"My dear," he said, "we Texans have grown so used to
fighting our own battles that doing anything else doesn't
come quite natural to us. But you're quite right, if I had been
here, I certainly would have advised against an independent
attack. Nevertheless, Texas, just because the largest ranches
haven't been touched . . . your father's and mine . . . is no
reason why we shouldn't concern ourselves about the misfortunes of our neighbors."

"Of course, we should concern ourselves. But we should
do it in the right way . . . by law."

"Yes, the law should come first, always," Orlando
Maxwell agreed.

"Your foreman, Saurel, is with them," said the girl, still

looking toward the oncoming group. "And there's a stranger."

"Yes, I see." The face of Orlando Maxwell had grown still more stern. "If Saurel took a leading part in this posse business, he'll hear from me."

The girl was not listening. "My, what a beauty," she breathed.

"What's that?"

"The horse the stranger is riding. Did you ever in your life see anything so perfect?"

The oncoming riders split up, the cowpunchers moving on to the corrals. Jim Hatfield, Sam Morgan, Sam Morgan's young foreman, Dave Horton, and Nash Saurel rode up to the porch.

"Light, Hatfield," Morgan said, "an' meet some folks. Hello, Texas. Hello, Orlando. You missed some excitement."

"Texas has been telling me something about it. What happened? Did the Comanches move out before you got there?"

"Jest a minute, Orlando, while I git the interdoocin' over with. This here is Jim Hatfield, a new hand I've taken on. This is my daughter, Texas. An' this is my neighbor an' very good friend, Orlando Maxwell."

"Pleased to meet you, Miss Texas," Hatfield said, taking the hand she held out to him. "Pleased to meet you, Mister Maxwell."

Orlando Maxwell didn't seem to notice the Ranger's extended hand, so Hatfield dropped it.

Kind of uppity, he thought. *Mebbe he don't make a practice o' bein' friendly with the hired help. Looks like a good man, though, to have alongside o' you in a fight. My new boss, Morgan, has got courage, but he's kind of mulish, but this one looks like an hombre that's got brains, education, and guts. Right now he seems to be angry in a quiet sort o' way. I reckon my good friend, Nash Saurel, is goin' to catch merry hell.*

Hatfield made quick mental notes of several things—it was his habit to do so.

Young Horton doesn't like this Maxwell. Easy to see why. Young Horton is kind o' sweet on Texas. Don't blame him much. She shore is a beauty. An' this Maxwell is kind of a strikin'- lookin' feller, the kind that could make a gal forgit he was twice her age . . . fer a time, anyway. Well, Cap McDowell says, always look an' listen. That's what I'm doin' now.

Meanwhile Sam Morgan was explaining what had happened.

"This stranger here," he was saying with a somewhat sheepish grin, "has sort o' took control o' things. I don't know jest how he managed it, but he seems to have a way with him. He put doubts in our minds that it was the Comanches. In fact, he went so far as to say it was Apaches."

"Apaches!" Maxwell exclaimed sharply. "How could a band of Apaches have come into this part of Texas without being noticed?"

"That's somethin' I haven't been able to figure out myself yet, Mister Maxwell," the Ranger answered.

"Well, anyway," continued Morgan, "the boys weren't quite satisfied. They wanted to ride over to the reservation anyhow. So we did. We rode clear into Morning Star's range. Nobody stopped us. An' square in the center of it, what do we see? There's a great circle o' Injun women and children. An' in the middle of it, walled round by 'em, is every gosh-danged Comanche warrior on the reservation. At first we couldn't believe our eyes. Comanche warriors. Hidin' behind their women and children! Well, we seen it was so. An' the funniest part was, they looked at us kind o' proudly, instead o' havin' their heads cast down. Just the same it shore looked comical.

Since we couldn't attack, there was only one thing left fer us to do an' that was to laugh. But this stranger here wouldn't even let us do that! 'The first man who laughs, I plug,' he calls out, an' he meant it. 'Those Comanches you see there know they ain't guilty, an' that they've got a right to defend themselves, but they also know that you *think* they're guilty. So they've chosen this way to prevent the sheddin' of innocent blood, yours as well as their own. It took a heap sight more courage to do what they're doin' than you could acquire in a thousand years. What you're seein' is nuthin' to laugh at, so don't laugh.'

"Well, we didn't. We rode away, an' here we are." Sam Morgan's face lost its good humor, became grave. "But the guilty parties has got to be punished!" he ended.

Orlando Maxwell was speaking. He was talking to Nash Saurel. His words snapped and crackled. The foreman seemed to wilt under the tongue-lashing. Help came from an unexpected source, Jim Hatfield.

"I wouldn't go fer blamin' Saurel such a powerful lot, Mister Maxwell. Cooler men than him wouldn't stop to think any more than he did, if they saw this . . . beggin' your pardon, miss. . . ." He held aloft the golden-haired scalp.

"Incidentally, it was this scalp that put me in mind o' the Apaches. Comanches cut from the hairline at the forehead, Apaches rip off a scalp startin' from the base o' the skull. That's the way this one was taken."

"You seem to know a great deal about Indians," Maxwell said with a hint of sarcasm in his voice.

"I traveled around a bit," the Lone Wolf answered. "I know a little o' this an' a little o' that."

Maxwell smiled thinly. "Sometimes a little knowledge is a dangerous thing. Anyway, I take it your theory is that the Apaches, committing those raids, staged things so as to make it look like the Comanches. Is that right?"

"So far, but there might be more to it than that. It don't pay to spin theories in advance o' the facts."

"You seem to be a kind of detective."

Hatfield grinned slightly. "No, I'm just a wanderin' cowpoke, lookin' fer a job."

"That's quite a horse for a wanderin' cowpoke to be riding."

"I raised him from a colt," Hatfield said simply.

"Would you care to sell him?"

"No, sir," Hatfield replied promptly.

"Mister Morgan's daughter here had expressed great admiration for him," Maxwell went on, and Hatfield noticed a dangerous flush rising on the face of Dave Horton. The girl noticed it, too, for there was a mischievous light in her eyes. "Texas knows that anything she wants, she can have, provided I have the power to give it. I wish to purchase the horse for her."

Apparently up to then Texas had thought Maxwell was joking. But now she knew he was speaking in earnest.

"No," she said quickly, "I won't hear of it, Mister Maxwell. Why, that horse must be worth a small fortune. . . ."

"Miss," Hatfield said quietly, "I'm not sellin', so there's no need for you to object so strenuously. If you don't mind, I'll be takin' my leave." With a bound he was in the saddle. "So long."

"Hey!" Sam Morgan cried out. "Where you goin'? I thought you was workin' fer me!"

Hatfield looked down at him. Before turning Goldy he spoke two words.

"I am."

He was gone like a streak of light. He couldn't forget the feeling that Orlando Maxwell had brewed in him. That proud, handsome face reeked with hate and distrust.

"Gosh," breathed Sam Morgan, his face perplexed and anxious, "you don't suppose he pulled the wool over my eyes, do you? You don't suppose it was the Comanches, after all?"

VI

Hatfield had not forgotten Devil's Pass. But Devil's Pass, he reasoned, would keep. The Lone Wolf decided that if the mountain massacre and the Indian raids were tied up together—and it was more than ever his hunch that they were—then it followed that the trail leading out of the pass and the trail leading away from the raids would meet somewhere and continue as a single trail. So, whichever of the two he took as his starting point, it would sooner or later set him on that single trail. That trail, he figured, would lead south, and he based this conclusion on his rapid observations made in flight from Devil's Pass.

Headlong as that flight had been, certain signs had not escaped his keen sight. They had told him that the thousands of cattle that had been driven into the pass had not come out again. The tracks had been plain, had pointed only one way, to the south. Those cattle had been driven out through the southern exit of the pass. But certain other animals, burros, *had* come out, and been driven back in again—they too had gone south.

And the Chisos Mountains are south, the Lone Wolf thought. *The Apaches are in the Chisos, have been fer the last two years. So there's no reason why I shouldn't head south, too. A visit to the Apaches seems to be in the cards. But there's one thing puzzles me, though.*

The thing that puzzled Jim was this: at the time that he had been sent out on his mission of peace to the Comanches, another Ranger, Bill Evans, had been sent on a similar mission to the Apaches. Assuming that Bill Evans had succeeded in his mission, why should there be any more reason for thinking that the Apaches would be guilty of those raids than there was for thinking that the Comanches were guilty.

The Comanches were *not* guilty. And the terms offered the Apaches had been fully as generous as those offered and accepted by the Comanches. The Apaches, therefore, had no more reason for perpetrating those raids than the Comanches had had.

I've got to get in touch with Cap'n McDowell, Hatfield thought. *I've got to know if he's heard from Bill Evans. Otherwise, my visit to the Apaches might be a waste o' time. An' time is one thing I can't afford to waste. I've kept cattlemen an' Comanches from makin' war on each other, but it's sort of a truce, it ain't real peace. I can't stay away from the Angela Mesa too long, but I can't afford to go back to the station, neither. So I'll have to telegraph.*

It was these thoughts that took Hatfield into Morrow, to the telegraph desk in the Wells Fargo office. He had a problem on his hands—to hide his identity and at the same time get a message through to Carson, from where it would be relayed to Captain McDowell. But the Lone Wolf had faced this same problem before and knew how to solve it.

Ranger messages, unless there was no need for concealment, were received in Carson by the town's undertaker and by him relayed to the station without delay. Accordingly Jim sent the following message:

Thornton,
Carson, Texas,
    Double play. Did B E make it? Reply at once Morrow.

The message was unsigned. "Double play" meant that Carson was to relay the message to Captain McDowell.

"I'll be back fer the answer in an hour," Hatfield said as he paid and walked out.

Since he had time to kill and was thirsty, the Ranger entered the Lone Star Saloon for a drink. As he raised the glass to his lips, he heard sounds of disturbance in the street. He set the whiskey down on the bar untasted. High-pitched yells, a series of shrill *yip-e-ees* punctuated by gunfire, penetrated the saloon.

"Sounds like some cowpokes have come into town fer a spree," said the bartender. "Hope they don't come in here an' start shootin' things up out o' sheer high spirits."

"You hoped wrong," Hatfield said, as half a dozen men pushed through the swinging doors. "Better keep your glassware under cover. They seem to be pretty much lit up already."

It was a typical group of waddies back from a long trail drive. They had been paid off; their pay was burning holes in their pockets.

"We ain't seed a bottle o' good ol' rotgut in six months!" the man who appeared to be the leading spirit of the six roared out. His staggering walk belied his words. "Bring out your best an' never mind the glasses! Never mind pullin' the corks, either! We'll bite off the necks of the bottles!"

He fired his six-gun into the ceiling. The others followed suit.

"*Yip-e-eeee!*"

At the sight of these antics, Hatfield's laughter had risen with the rest—the West was tolerant of such behavior. Then all in an instant Hatfield's expression changed; the humorous glints in his eyes became points of deadly fire; one of his guns was in his hand as though it had leaped from its holster of

itself; flame spurted from it, a bullet sped, and one of the rois-
terers, the leader, was dropped. Hatfield wasted no time. He
was in grave trouble and he knew it. He vaulted the bar and
took shelter behind it. As he did so, the bartender grappled
with him.

"You killer," the bartender panted. "He was drunk.
They're jest cowpokes in fer a spree!"

Hatfield shot up his free hand and seized an empty
whiskey bottle. He did not want to kill this man if he could
help it, since his sentiments sounded sincere, but it was necessary to get him out of the way for the time being. Hatfield
swung his arm down and brought the bottle to rest with a
stunning blow on the bartender's head. The bartender col-
lapsed with a groan and lay still.

Cowpokes in for a spree, hey? Hatfield thought feverishly.
*Fine way to kill a man an' call it an accident. Reckon folks didn't
notice, like I did, how their aim was comin' down. Fer a minute I
couldn't even believe it myself. Then, when I saw the look in that
varmint's eyes . . . hell, his eyes showed what his hand was goin' to
do. This is a tough spot. I'll have the whole place against me, with
their thinkin' I killed a happy cowpoke wanton-like. . . .*

All these thoughts flashed through the Lone Wolf's mind
in the space of a second. He had no time to ask himself what
or who could be behind this attempt upon his life. A knife
came flying over the counter, shattering some of the bottles
on the shelf above him.

That must have been the Mex-lookin' gent who's with 'em, he
thought. *I reckon I could get out of this if I flashed my badge.
Then the crowd'd be with me. At that, maybe they wouldn't. Not
unless I could convince 'em that those gents came in to do murder.
Nope, my badge stays where it is. It ain't time to flash it yet.
There's still too much I don't know. I've got to make five corpses
before I get out o' here. That's bad, because dead men can't talk,*

but I reckon I've got trouble enough gettin' myself out o' this without tryin' to take one o' them varmints alive.

The Ranger raised himself for a quick look, but immediately jerked himself down again. Bullets whizzed over the bar and into the shelves behind it. Nevertheless, his darting glance had given him a rough notion of what the situation was.

The regular patrons of the saloon had taken refuge as soon as they had seen horseplay turn to deadly earnest—behind chairs, tables, the faro layout, anything they could find. But six men had remained in the open. One because he lay stiffly in death, the others with their guns out.

"Do they look drunk now!" Jim Hatfield shouted. "Take a squint at the varmints! Do they look drunk now? They came in here to kill me! If I hadn't done what I did, I'd be dead right now!"

"You're goin' to be!" a voice bellowed. "No, we ain't drunk now! We was, but we ain't no more! Your killin' our pard has made us sober! Come out an' take what's comin' to you!"

That varmint's a quick thinker, Hatfield thought. Aloud he called: "Come an' get me!"

There was a pound of heavy feet across the floor, a frantic curse. A shape came plunging over the bar. There was the clatter of metal on the floor as the assailant lost his gun. But apparently he didn't need it, for he was a man of enormous strength, with strength increased tenfold by rage and hate. His hairy arms shot out, clutched, jerked the Ranger toward him.

Hatfield let himself be drawn in. But his right hand still held his gun; the heel of that hand was pressed against his own chest, so that the gun barrel stuck out straight. He felt it meet the flesh of his assailant's midriff, felt it sink in, triggered. Smoke, blood, and flesh all mingled together—with a frightful cry the enormous hulk fell away from Jim.

Deprived of this shelter, Hatfield's gaze rose only just in time. A face showed through the gunsmoke, a gun barrel appeared. The Ranger sent his iron up without waste motion in a short sharp angle. It stopped and spat lead simultaneously. The flame seemed almost to leap out and lick the looming face, which became an unrecognizable smear of blood as the body slumped out of sight on the other side of the bar.

Something crashed into the wall behind the Lone Wolf. He turned for a quick look. It was another knife, stuck deeply, still quivering with the force of the impact. The Mexican again.

The angle from which the knife had been thrown puzzled Hatfield. He saw that it couldn't have been thrown by a man standing on the floor of the Lone Star—in that case it could never have cleared the bar. It had come down diagonally, from a height. Moreover, it had not come straight but from somewhere off to the side.

He took another quick look, figured in a flash the vertical angle, the lateral angle, calculated at the same time the spot in the saloon from which the knife must have come, and on the strength of that calculation sprang erect and triggered almost before his eyes had time to tell him that his brain had figured it out correctly.

Between the spitting of the first and second bullet, in that split second, he saw a stepladder off to the side somewhat, the Mexican upon it, the Mexican tumbling off it, dead before he hit the floor.

Two of 'em left, he thought grimly as he cleared his eyes of the sweat that was pouring off his brow. As things stood, he was a prisoner behind that bar.

Hatfield knew a situation like this couldn't last; sooner or later it would have to break up. Either he or they would have to make a move, and there was no guarantee that the man who moved first would come out on top. There was no telling what was taking place on the other side unless he raised himself, and, if he raised himself, he exposed himself. He had done that before, but if he did it again, it might be once too often.

Keen as Hatfield's hearing was, it couldn't tell him much. He heard labored breathing and judged that it came from the two survivors, but he couldn't be sure. He couldn't risk rising and throwing a couple of quick bullets in the direction from which the sounds were coming. What had worked with the Mexican might not work a second time. The law of averages was against him.

His throat felt parched and his lungs were hot with gunsmoke and the stench of liquor from the numerous broken bottles. He found himself fighting down a sudden overmastering desire for water. The tap was near and there was a glass beneath it, but he didn't dare risk taking what might be his last drink.

Then, in a flash, he was in rapid action again. He picked up bottles, one after another; full ones, empty ones, broken ones. He hurled them over the bar. He lay down a barrage of bottles, not seeing where they struck, only knowing that the barrage might give him the chance he depended on. Then, as suddenly as he had started the barrage, he stopped it. He darted along parallel to the bar swiftly, quietly toward the bar's end, near the entrance of the Lone Star.

Still in a crouch he swung around it. He saw the two jerk sidewise toward him, startled. He came in low. Their first bullets whizzed over his head, but he had begun to trigger almost as soon as he had made the turn. He threw lead as fast as his trigger fingers could obey his sight.

Each time the bullet sped from below upward, guided by a wrist and an eye as sensitive to angles as a steel needle is sensitive to the magnetic pole. Not a bullet missed, yet they remained incredibly on their feet. But it was impossible for Hatfield, in the speed with which he had to act, to succeed in disabling without hitting any vital spot. No, he would never get any information from these two. He saw them wilt, saw their knees cave, saw the savage expressions on the stubble-grown faces change to the look of men who know, in that horrible second of consciousness before the end, that they are dying. Blood welled up out of their throats, came out of their mouths, and they sank to the floor.

Cold sweat covered Jim, but he moved backward to the bar, his guns still leveled. He surveyed the scene. The sudden silence was breathtaking. He judged it safe to replace one gun in its holster. His free arm then went back and his fingers curled about a glass of whiskey. It was the drink he had ordered when he had first entered the saloon. Through all the battle and carnage it had remained miraculously untouched.

Hatfield gulped it down. It seemed to taste of gunsmoke but it heartened him. He looked around him. The saloon was a shambles. Broken glass lay everywhere and the floor was soaked with liquor and blood.

"You can all come out now," he said. "There'll be no more shootin'."

The Lone Star's patrons came out hesitantly. Hatfield eyed them.

"Some o' you," he said, "may still be uncertain about the rights an' wrongs o' this business. The facts are simple. They made out they were drunk an' they weren't drunk. They made out they were shootin' off innocent fireworks, like cowpokes will do when they come into town fer a spree, but they

113

began givin' a direction to their bullets that wasn't innocent, with me as the unwilling target. The second point ain't any longer accessible to proof, exceptin' my word, but the first point can be readily checked. Any o' you gents is free to smell their breaths, if you're interested."

Someone laughed raucously, but there was a frightened note to the laughter. "They ain't got no breaths left to smell," this one said.

Hatfield's face hardened. "I killed because I had to," he said. "I ain't laughin' about it."

The laugher looked scared. "Shore," he said hastily, "I wasn't meanin' to laugh."

"Well, suppose you volunteer then," the Ranger said.

"Not me, stranger. I believe you without that. Not me."

Another man stepped forward. "I'll do it," he said.

Startled, Jim Hatfield recognized him. It was Vance Thompson. Apparently, Hatfield thought, the young and now jobless foreman wanted to make up to him for the insult he had leveled that morning.

Vance Thompson knelt beside each corpse in turn. Had he not been so deeply tanned his face would have been seen to grow progressively paler as he proceeded with the examination. At the end he arose looking a bit sick.

"Not a breath o' liquor on any one o' them," he announced.

"Why was they gunnin' for you, stranger?" someone asked.

Hatfield made no answer. "Thanks," he said to Thompson. "It wasn't a pleasant chore, I know. But would you mind searchin' 'em fer me? I'm kinda interested in who they were." He spoke this last in a low voice.

"Don't you know?" Thompson asked in surprise, his own voice equally low.

"No, do you?"

"No, but I thought that you. . . ."

"You thought that, since I killed 'em, I must've known 'em. It doesn't always follow like that. I'd like you to tell Sam Morgan, over at the Circle Seven, about what happened here."

"Ain't you goin' back there yourself. I thought you was workin' fer him."

"Tell him I still am, but don't tell that to anyone else. An' tell him I said to give you a job. Now go ahead with the search."

The search yielded little of value for purposes of identification.

"I ain't stealin'," Hatfield informed the Lone Star's patrons while it was proceeding.

"Nobody said you were," was the hasty reply.

The corpses yielded up some tobacco, brown papers, and about 100 silver dollars in all.

"Mexican dollars," Hatfield muttered, examining them. "State of Coahuila. This is the governor of Coahuila's picture stamped on 'em. What's his name again? I recollect . . . Alvarez."

Alvarez. The name tantalized him. He had the feeling that he had either heard or seen it before, recently. Suddenly, with a thrill, it came to him. It had been one of the names signed to that bloody shirt. José Alvarez. But the Coahuila governor's name was Guillermo. Yes, that was true, but he had two brothers. Jim, who made it his business to know a little of everything, had some knowledge of Mexican politics.

Alvarez, he thought. *Devil's Pass. I stop an Indian war an' six varmints come gunnin' fer me. An' they've got Coahuila money on 'em. My hunch was right. All this business connects.*

"This money will go to the undertaker fer the burial o'

these men," he announced, placing it on the bar. "Come on, Thompson."

Outside, with the puzzled Vance Thompson beside him, he mounted Goldy and they rode the short distance to the Wells Fargo office. The telegraph operator saw them through the window and came out.

"Heard sounds like cowpokes in for a spree," he said. "They seem to have quieted themselves down. What happened? Did they drink themselves to sleep? Here's your answer. It came in only a minute ago."

Hatfield took the message from him. It was short.

J. H. Morrow,
B.E. overdue. No word. Worried.

That was all, but it told the Lone Wolf what his next step must be.

The longest way around is sometimes the shortest way home, he thought. *I'm takin' it. I reckon Bill's dead, otherwise Cap would've heard from him. Reckon he was stopped before he ever reached the Apaches. Someone was anxious that the Apaches should never know about the treaty he had fer them. The same someone as was responsible fer Devil's Pass an' the Comanche raids.* "Git goin', Goldy. We're headin' our noses south."

Jim Hatfield was mistaken—Bill Evans was not dead. High up in the sinister jumble of the Chisos, backing up a knife-edge ridge that flanked a ravine, was a cave that had once been inhabited by a mountain lion. Bill Evans lived in that cave, had been living in it for eleven days and eleven nights. The mountain lion was gone. For eleven days that mountain lion had been going into Bill Evans's stomach.

On the ridge was other meat of a different kind. Buzzards

were feeding on it. It was the meat of human beings. Evidence of past feedings was to be seen in several skeletons. There was also the partially devoured body of a horse—Bill's horse.

The sun rose on the twelfth day of the siege. Bill looked out from the mouth of the cave. The ridge was quiet, except for the sound of the buzzards feeding. But Bill knew it would not remain quiet for long.

This twelfth day promised to be his last. Not because he believed the men who had been besieging him would succeed in getting him on this particular day, but because of his diet of meat. Straight meat, coupled with insufficient water, was having its effect on him—he was losing strength at a rapid rate.

A grim smile twisted his lips. He had made them pay plenty in advance for his own inevitable death. He knew that not all the men he had killed lay on the ridge. Some of them had tumbled into the ravine. Who his besiegers were he did not know. He could only guess that the siege had something to do with the treaty, written in both English and the Athapascan dialect, which he bore on his person.

His eyes glowed with fever; his ordinarily clean-shaven face was bearded. Looking at the buzzards engaged in their disgusting feeding, he shuddered.

Reckon Si Parker will never blow taps over my grave, he thought. *Now, if it was eagles, I wouldn't mind so much. But buzzards is so far an' away the lowest scum o' creation that even a rattlesnake is noble by comparison. No bullets left fer my six-guns. Only a few cartridges fer my rifle, but they ain't gonna kill me.*

Evans rolled over on his side and his thoughts rambled on: *When they figger my last bullet is gone an' they come in fer me, I'll sink my knife in the first one's ribs an' then jest let go, jest die. But it'll be my doin', not theirs. The way I feel now, I reckon all I got to do to die is jest give myself the word.*

His blood-shot eyes sharpened. "The day's work is beginnin'," he muttered. He had seen the buzzards suddenly rise with a frightened flutter. That meant that his unseen enemies were bestirring themselves. At least one of them had come onto the ridge.

Bill Evans did not see him. He never saw any of them first off. The ridge did not make an even ascent; it rose to the mouth of the cave in a series of what might be called steps, sharp inclines alternating with level ground. Evans usually caught sight of the approaching enemy on the third of those steps. But now the human débris on the ridge provided additional shelter for the attackers. As the siege lengthened, they had been able to get closer and closer.

The sun was Bill Evans's ally. The human bodies cast shadows, and Bill had learned the trick of calculating the location of the body from the shadow, and from that figuring in advance the instant when the body itself was likely to come into sight. This morning, however, the Ranger's growing weakness prevented his brain from making the calculation on time.

There was a sudden rattle of gunfire from below. Bullets kicked up rocky splinters, shot sparks from the ground at the mouth of the cave. One of the splinters was driven into Bill's cheek, but he paid no heed to the trickling blood. Carefully he sighted his rifle, waited, saw his target, deflected his aim the least bit, and triggered.

There was no answering cry to indicate that his bullet had found its target, but he heard a splash as of a body falling into shallow water. That meant that the body had rolled off the ridge.

Evans's heart swelled in bitter exultation. *It's a fort,* he thought for the hundredth time. *This place is a fort. With enough ammunition, water to drink, an' sufficient grub, I could* hold off an army here until I was an old man. But that cat meat has made me sick, and I got no more water, nor bullets beyond what's in the chambers now. I got the fort, but I ain't got the strength or material to hold it. I reckon it's the finish.

He felt his body burning, and his heart was pounding more cruelly. There was a terrible light in his eyes, as if in response to the tumultuous thoughts that had suddenly begun to rage within him. He had an uncontrollable impulse to shout out his defiance in the face of impending death—to shout out his heart's hate to the unknown men who besieged him, the mountains that hemmed him in, the buzzards that promised to be his only grave.

His Adam's apple jerked convulsively as his thoughts roared up out of his throat and found vent. With a contorted face, knowing his own death could not be far off, but triumphant in the knowledge that he had done his job for as long as he had been able, he sent his voice roaring out of the cave and down the ridge. His fever gave him eloquence.

"White-livered varmints! Sons-o'-bitches! How many of you does it take to get one man? You come crawlin' at me like rattlesnakes, but a rattlesnake is better than you . . . he rattles before he strikes! A buzzard is better than you . . . he cleans up after him! You was too ornery, low-down to take care o' your own dead. You wouldn't risk haulin' 'em away fer burial. An' I would've let you do it! Yes, if I'd've seen *that* was what you wanted, I would've held my fire! But you used 'em to hide behind while spittin' your lead up at me. You chose to leave 'em fer the buzzards to pick clean! Well, come on up an' see how many more of you will make meals fer hell birds! I'm only one man! Not a hundred, not ten, only one! But you'll never get me! You'll never. . . ."

He stopped short, an aghast look on his face. An answer had come.

It was not the answer of gunfire. It was a voice. A voice had answered him. And it was one that he knew well. He could not believe it. His fever must be playing tricks on him. A thrill ran through him from his head to his feet, the sharpest, gladdest thrill he had ever known. That voice!

"Hold the fort, Bill!" the voice came up the ridge, and it was like the clanging of a great bell ringing out good tidings. "Hang on! Ride 'em down, Goldy!"

An apparition had burst in upon the besiegers. It was an apparition in two parts, a horse and a rider. The suddenness of their coming made them loom all the more gigantic and terrible in the eyes of men who for eleven days had been pointing their desires only one way—upward to the cave. But the suddenness of this visitation from behind them was as nothing compared to its violence.

The rider on that golden horse seemed to possess six hands, so rapidly did fire come spurting from his guns. He seemed to have dropped down from the sky, bringing his own thunderstorm with him, so deafening were the close-range reports, so lightning-like the flames that shot from the mouths of the black muzzles. And what he didn't do, his horse did. It whirled, this way and that, responsive to the mere pressure of its rider's knees, leaving his deadly hands free to deal out certain death.

"Stomp him, Goldy!" the rider roared, and the golden horse reared up for the man that was under him was in that instant nothing but a cry, a strangled, terror-stricken cry. The golden horse came down, his hoofs crushing, killing everything that was in his path. There was a sudden silence, as though a storm had come to an abrupt end.

The rider's work had been like an avenging angel's, as swift and as sure. Only the voice of Bill Evans, calling to the man who had saved him, broke the stillness—which was intensified by the murmur of the brook that ran in the ravine below.

"Stay where you are, Bill!" Jim Hatfield shouted back. "I'm comin' up!"

Hatfield picked his way up the ridge, past the bodies and the bones, past the carcass of Bill Evans's horse. He dismounted at the mouth of the cave. Evans tried to get up, but weakness overcame him. He could only sit and grin up at Jim Hatfield out of his beard.

"Jim," he said huskily, "you ol' son."

The Lone Wolf took one look at him, said—"Glad to see you, Bill."—went out to Goldy and came back with his canteen. "Drink, Bill," he said, his face drawn with worry. "Not too much, son. Jest a little at a time."

Bill drank. Hatfield coughed and looked around the cave. "Nice little home you got here," he said, glancing around, "but I reckon it needs a little cleanin' up."

He dragged the remains of the mountain lion's carcass out of the cave and flung it over the ledge. When he came back, he made bacon and coffee.

"Don't talk yet," he said. "Eat."

Bill Evans ate, and, while he ate, the man whose keen eyes missed nothing, busied himself with binding up his ankle. The strong fingers that could twirl six-guns as if they were toys were gentle as a woman's as they felt of the injury.

"Broken," he murmured, "but mending. I reckon you been off it fer a spell."

Evans grinned. "Them varmints wouldn't let me take no walks," he said. "Jim, I still can't believe it. I thought I was a goner fer shore. Then you happen along. How come?"

"I heard shots," Hatfield explained simply. "So I come up behind the spot where I judged they was comin' from. Allus a good policy when you don't know who's doin' the shootin'.

An' I get a pretty good view of the proceedin's without bein' seen myself. Well, at first I didn't know what to make of it. There were half a dozen *hombres* gunnin' fer someone in a cave was all that I knew. I didn't know that someone was you, an' for a moment I thought those *hombres* might be peace officers, though they didn't look much like it. Then I heard your voice. Gosh, my spine is still pricklin' with the memory o' that."

"Your feelin' at hearin' my voice ain't nuthin' to what I felt when I heard yours," Evans said. "But you ain't yet told me, Jim, how do you happen to be in this neck o' the woods in the first place?"

"That can wait," Hatfield said. "From the looks o' things, you've been in this spot fer quite a spell, standin' off that siege. How in all tarnation did you do it? What happened?"

Bill Evans smiled weakly and started his story.

"This is the twelfth day, Jim. I'm twelve days older, or twelve years, since me an' my hoss tumbled off the upper ledge, with a bullet in him. I can't say I know the why of it. I only know I was ridin' peaceable when a shot came an' it sent me flying. The rest is a kind of jumble. My hoss was killed, but by some miracle I got nuthin' but a busted ankle. After I fell, I could hear other hosses snortin' up above an' I figured I better take cover. I saw the opening of this cave, an' I crawled toward it as fast as I could. But I found it wasn't empty. It had a tenant. That mountain cat came at me spittin'. I had one o' my guns out, though I don't remember drawin' it, an' I blew out the cat's brains with one quick shot. Its blood spattered over me, but I crawled in, turned around, an' waited fer what was to come.

"Two things helped me . . . it was along toward sunset an' this cave is set in kind o' deep, so that there's a sort o' ceilin' o' rock over the entrance. That made a bad angle fer the varmints who were tryin' to get me. They had to go down and get at me from the bottom o' the ridge. That sort o' placed them in an exposed position. I got two of 'em . . . they're picked bones now. They don't believe in burying. Night came on an' I realized I was goin' to be here fer a spell. I had nuthin' but my two guns an' my knife. My canteens, saddlebags, rifle, an' rope were out on the ridge with my dead hoss.

"I waited. Soon I heard the sound o' someone crawlin' up toward the cave. I waited, then I fired at the sound. It was a lucky shot an' I heard a death rattle. That stopped 'em . . . fer a time. I waited a while longer an' then I crawled out. I brought back my belongin's. Well, that was eleven nights ago. I've been on a diet of raw cat ever since. You've seen what you've seen and I don't have to tell you what the rest was like."

"But what did you do fer water?" Jim asked. "One canteen couldn't have lasted you all that time."

"It didn't. That's where my rope came in. I used to crawl out at night and lower the canteen to the brook. I couldn't do it often, it was too risky, so I've been on short water rations right along."

"An' how about sleep?" Hatfield asked. "How is it they didn't get you while you were sleepin'?"

"Again the rope. An' again I worked at night. I strung up a sort o' barrier, startin' where my hoss was. I attached my end of it to my hand, usin' a slipknot because I didn't want to be jerked out o' the cave by anyone who took hold of the other end. They never did, though. I figger they never knew about the rope. They used to stumble over piles o' stones I'd set out, but they never knew in the dark that they'd been set there. An' whenever they'd come up against the hoss to climb it, I'd feel the jerk an' give 'em lead. It worked, but I never had any real sleep fer all o' that."

"You finished off quite a few o' them," Hatfield said. "That sort o' puzzles me. They don't seem to have showed much sense. All they had to do was jest stay there, down below, an' wait fer you to starve."

There was not much mirth in Bill's grin. "I sort o' figured they'd come around to that way o' thinkin'," he said. "That they'd jest sit back an' wait fer thirst an' hunger to do the job fer them, but I wouldn't let 'em."

"How could you prevent it?"

"I made 'em mad. I yelled down at 'em in terms that wasn't complimentary. I said things that no man will take from anyone. I goaded them into comin' at me. I figgered it was my only chance . . . to kill them all off. Up to a certain point it worked. But if it wasn't fer you. . . ."

Bill's voice trailed off, and, when he began again, there was a trace of moisture in his eyes. "I don't want to talk about it any more," he said. "I want to forget it. Tell me how you come to be here. That'll be more interestin'."

VII

Hatfield did not press Bill Evans further. For a moment he was silent, thinking, mentally going back over what had happened.

"Bill," he said at last, "I'll tell you as much I know. Two heads are better than one, an' maybe, as I talk to you, things will grow a mite clearer. Usually I've got only Goldy to listen to me, an' Goldy's a good listener, but it ain't quite the same as talkin' to a feller human. It's true Goldy kin all but talk, but the fact remains he stops short o' that, an' sometimes an *hombre* wants an answer from a human tongue."

"Fire away," said Bill Evans, "an' I'll do my best to give you the benefit o' what little hoss sense my brains has got left. But first would you mind rollin' me a brain tablet. I kin use it."

Hatfield complied. "It wasn't any accident that brought me here," he said thoughtfully, as Evans gratefully exhaled his first puff. "It's true I come a long way 'round, which took time, but I'm convinced I never really left the trail I should be followin'. In other words, I may think I'm lost an' off the trail, but I really ain't."

"Sounds to me like you're talkin' to yourself even though you ain't alone," Evans said. "You may be follerin' that trail you're talkin' about but I'm sure not follerin' you."

"First there's Devil's Pass," Hatfield said. He told Bill about what had happened there, showed him the shirt, described his own escape. "In takin' Ned back to the station, I thought I was leavin' the trail. Without Ned on my hands, I

125

would've worked out from Devil's Pass direct. But it couldn't be helped, I said to myself. Ned had to be buried, an' Devil's Pass would have to wait. So I took him back. Funny thing is, if I hadn't done that, I wouldn't be here. So I reckon I got no cause to complain."

Evans stared at him, wide-eyed.

"*You* got no cause to complain? Reckon I'm the one that's got no complaint to make on that score! Gosh, if you hadn't come, I'd've been dead by now. But how come your goin' back to the station resulted in bringin' you here?" Evans asked.

"I'm comin' to that. As I say, when I left Devil's Pass, I thought I was leavin' the trail I should be follerin'. Nevertheless, in all that's happened since then, I've felt that I never really left the trail. When I got back to the station, Cap'n McDowell told me the Comanches was raidin'."

Evans's mouth dropped open.

"Shore," Hatfield said. "You're as surprised to hear that as I was, an' I shore was surprised, seein' as I'd jest successfully concluded a peace treaty with Morning Star."

"But . . . ?"

"It wasn't the Comanches . . . it was Apaches. That's where you come in."

"Keep talkin'," Evans said. "This is gettin' pow'ful interestin'."

"I made tracks fer the Great Angela Mesa, where the trouble was. The ranchers there were gettin' ready to clean the Comanches out o' Texas once and for all. I stopped that, or anyway postponed it. All right. It wasn't Comanches, it was Apaches. But if it wasn't Comanches, on account of the treaty I'd made with them an' fer other reasons, how could it be Apaches when *you'd* been sent to make the same kind o' treaty with *them?* There was only one answer to that . . . you hadn't made the treaty. I telegraphed the Cap'n. He telegraphed back that he hadn't heard from you. That settled it. I had to come look fer you. But before I got Cap's answer, somethin' else happened."

The Lone Wolf told Bill Evans about the events in the saloon in Morrow. "The two things . . . my stoppin' an Indian war an' the attempt on my life . . . came too close together fer there not to be a connection between them. Someone knew how to strike an' strike fast. So that's why I left Morrow an' headed this way."

"Seems to me that Ned an' me have been gettin' in your way," Evans murmured in low tones.

"No," said Hatfield. "You fit right into all of this. You were stopped because you were in somebody's way. Somebody needed the Apaches fer the dirty work that was done on the mesa, an' he couldn't't've got them if you'd've got to them first with the treaty. They, not knowin' about the treaty, was somehow persuaded to execute those raids. Then the blame was thrown on the Comanches fer burnin' up six ranches. The range was gettin' ready to fight on account of it when I came along. An' I reckon that jest suited somebody's purpose, not my comin' along, of course, but the clean-up of the Indians."

"But why?" the injured Ranger asked. "What did anyone have to gain . . . ?"

"Land, I expect," Hatfield said soberly. "Indian land an' burned-out land o' raided spreads. That's what it seems to shape up to so far, leastwise so far as the happenings on the mesa are concerned. Someone wants land, plenty of it, an' there's no reason fer thinkin' that, if he wants what the Comanches have got an' are goin' to get, he doesn't want still more. Mebbe he wants the hull mesa . . . mebbe even all o' Texas."

"Gosh," Evans said. "I kin see the first part of it . . . but all o' Texas? What makes you say a thing like that?"

Hatfield's eyes were bleak and the lines about his wide mouth had grown grim. "The varmint that could plan an' execute that massacre in Devil's Pass," he said in a low voice, almost as though he were talking to himself, "is no ordinary *hombre*. That kind of man dreams big, aims high, an' acts without conscience."

"Reckon you're right enough about that," Evans said, a puzzled look on his face, "but I don't exactly see the tie-up between Devil's Pass an' the happenings on the mesa. What makes you so shore there's a connection?"

"The method," Hatfield said. "In Devil's Pass, John Holcomb's men an' José Alvarez's men killed each other. But the first shots didn't come from them, they only thought they did. Someone made them think so, an' that someone, after those first shots, didn't have to lift a finger to help the massacre along. In other words, that someone worked out a method o' gettin' other men to kill each other off an' save him all the danger an' trouble o' doin' it himself. What he succeeded in doin' in Devil's Pass, he tried to repeat on the Mesa, with Indians this time instead o' Mexicans. If you'll stop to think about it, you'll see one great advantage in the method right away . . . it doesn't require a large force o' men to execute it, an' the fewer men, the less chance o' the conspiracy comin' to light by someone talkin' careless. Oh, there's a lot I don't know, but Devil's Pass an' the mesa tie in, I don't doubt it for a minute."

"But all o' Texas," Evans muttered, still wondering about that amazing statement of Hatfield's. "I can't see that. . . ."

"It's wild," Hatfield agreed. "I don't know as I kin justify that thought by any reasonable figurin'. . . ." His voice trailed off for a moment while he thought. "Unless," he murmured, as he returned mentally to his surroundings, "unless this business has got roots in other places besides Texas . . . in Mexico mebbe." The idea hung fire for a few silent minutes, then Hatfield continued. "Texas was once Mexican territory. There's no reason fer thinkin' that Mexicans . . . some o' them anyway . . . don't want it back, or if they don't get that idea by themselves, someone in Texas, someone who's responsible fer what's been happenin' *in* Texas, couldn't give 'em that idea, an' get the help he needed that way. Why, what's the matter, Bill? You look. . . ."

The blood had completely left Bill Evans's face. He was staring at the Lone Wolf like a man in a trance. At last he managed to croak: "You mean another Mexican War?"

Hatfield had reached over to feel his pulse, but Bill Evans threw off his hand. "I'm all right!" he cried. "Only I jist remembered something I saw this morning. Curse me fer a forgettin' fool, but all the excitement, the fight, your comin' when you did, clean druv it out o' my no-account brains!"

"What is it, Bill?"

"Dig into my saddlebags an' take out my field glasses."

"What for?" Hatfield asked, then checked his curiosity and said soothingly, imagining that Bill Evans's fever was increasing and that as a consequence it would be best to humor him. "Shore, shore. Jest a minute."

"I want you to take a look at somethin'," Evans said, his voice growing calmer. "You know, since this was my home fer so long, I sort've got to know it purty well. We're on a high up spot, Jim. Well, there's sort of an openin' in the back wall o' this cave, enough to see through anyway. I used to look through it on them rare occasions when those varmints was restin'. I got plumb tired o' the front view, seein' as in a few days I could call every rock by its name. Damned if I couldn't see the Río rollin' far away there, to the south. This mornin', at sunup, I took another look. It was little innocent diversions like that kept me from goin' loco. An' this mornin' I seed a pile o' horsemen crossin' the Río into Texas . . . a few hundred of 'em they was. After what you told me 'bout that Mex money, an' Devil's Pass, an' now a possible Mexican War . . . my God, Jim!" His voice rose again, but now his cheeks were hot with the crimson glow of fever.

"Easy, Bill," Hatfield said, going to the back of the cave with the glasses.

"No sign of 'em now," the Lone Wolf said after a minute of looking. To himself he thought: *Shouldn't be surprised if it was only Bill's imagination, with his fever an' all. His hand was mighty hot an' his pulse was racin'. Reckon what I said about a Mexican War set his mind goin' backward sort of. Still, I'm takin' nuthin' fer granted. Bill says he saw 'em, an' maybe he did.* He turned. No sound came from Bill Evans. Alarmed, Hatfield went to him. But Evans had simply fallen asleep. The Ranger's face softened. He knew that for the first time in days Bill Evans was sleeping soundly.

"Sleep," he muttered. "You've earned it. I kin wait."

Hatfield got out the makings and smoked the time away. He took stock of what had happened and of the rôle he had been playing. It was a queer sort of rôle.

It seems to me, he thought to himself, *that what I've been doin' up to now, without exactly knowin' how an' why, is a sort o' gettin' in someone's way . . . stoppin' things before they start, you might say. Devil's Pass . . . well, that I couldn't stop. But someone was interested in stirrin' up a range war that would end with the Comanches bein' swept out o' Texas. I stopped that. Someone must've made some tall promises to the Apaches to get them to help in the job. But all the promises in the world, true or false, wouldn't have worked if the Apaches knew about the treaty. And Bill was stopped. That brings me up to date. Now I got to wait fer Bill to wake up. Then I'll pay my visit to the Apaches an' see what that brings. After that, I'll look into this business Bill was talking about . . . those* hombres crossin' *the Rio from old Mexico. It begins to look like this business has its roots in Mexico.*

Bill woke up at noon, shame-faced at having fallen asleep. He seemed to have forgotten what they had last spoken about. "Tarnation," he said, "I've been wastin' your time, Jim."

"No, you haven't. I've been thinkin'."

"Jim," Evans said, "I ain't goin' with you. You can't afford to be saddled with an invalid like me. I'd cramp you an' get in your way. You've got too much to do, too much territory to cover. Besides, you allus work best alone. Ain't that so, Lone Wolf?"

Hatfield was silent. He thought of Ned Markham and of how he had had to bear Ned's body homeward. Ned had been dead. Could he do less for Bill, who was alive?

"What do you want me to do, Bill?" he suddenly burst out. "Leave you here? There's hosses down below, the hosses that belonged to them varmints. I'll bring one of 'em up. You kin set a hoss, I reckon. I ain't gonna leave you, Bill. Maybe I should, but I can't."

"Tell you what you do, Jim," Evans said, his voice unsteady. "Go to the Apaches with the treaty an' then come back fer me. See what's what first. I'm ashamed to say it, but I ain't fit fer travelin' yet. Mebbe you kin work out a plan, so's I kin rest up somewheres in safety, an' you'll be free to act on your own. You can't fool me, Jim. You're all restless an' impatient inside. I'm in your way."

"A man who's done what you've done doesn't need to be ashamed of anything," Hatfield replied gruffly. "All right, I'll leave you. But I'll be back. I'll be back if I have to tear down these mountains to get to you."

He spoke confidently, but his heart was heavy. The portions of Bill Evans's face not covered by his beard, tanned as they were, revealed the telltale greenish pallor beneath. Ranger Evans needed a soft bed, nourishing food, complete rest. The meat of that mountain lion had poisoned him. And Jim Hatfield understood that Bill Evans was fully aware of how sick he was, but that nevertheless he was sending him away to do his job.

How can I be shore I'll be back in time? Hatfield thought. *How can I tell in advance what might happen to delay me? In another minute we'll be sayin' good bye to each other, an' he'll know that it may be fer the last time, an' I'll know it, too. But his thoughts won't show in his face. He'll make out he's OK. An' all the while we'll both be knowin' the truth . . . that Bill Evans is dyin' because nobody kin give him the care he needs. Ain't there some other way? Ain't there some other way?*

VIII

Suddenly Hatfield stiffened. "Look down there," he said to Bill tensely. "It looks like I ain't leavin' you fer yet a while."

Bill Evans followed the direction of Hatfield's gaze. His face grew even more mottled. What Jim had first noticed was a movement in the tall grass that grew in a sort of bowl-shaped plateau about a quarter of a mile below. Several times, while Bill had been asleep, his gaze had rested upon it, and he had wondered idly how it had come to grow in such a rocky and inhospitable surroundings.

It was good to see green among so much sinister gray, to watch the play of sunlight and shadow on it while the wind imparted to it a wave-like motion—the wind that must have at some time blown the first seeds to the forbidden spot and caused the grass to grow there. It was not these things that had caused Hatfield to grow tense. His keen eyes had noticed something unnatural in the behavior of the grass. He had seen it bending against the wind. Grass did not behave that way unless a counterforce was being exerted from the opposite direction—in this case it had to be animal or human, and Hatfield had quickly seen that it was human. He saw first one head and then another, yet a third. And all at once Bill Evans and he were seeing more than a score of moving shapes, darting like shadows from rock to rock, advancing.

"Apaches," the Lone Wolf said briefly. "An' a couple o' whites."

"Jim," Bill Evans said bleakly, "it's goin' to begin all over again. You've got to git out o' here. There's still time. You kin fork Goldy an' cut 'round the foot o' the ridge before they get too close. There's a slash up there that Goldy kin jump an' then you'll be in the clear. I don't count no more, Jim. I didn't want to say it before, but now I say it. There ain't enough life left in me to save, an', if you stay here, you'll only have to go through what I went through. There won't even be a dead cat fer you to eat, an' I know you'd sooner starve than kill Goldy. I'm only one *hombre*. You can't stop what you're doin' fer the sake of one *hombre*, 'specially since it wouldn't do no good in my case anyhow an' might end in you cashin' in your checks, too. Fork out o' here, Jim. Please!"

"Shut up, Bill," said the Lone Wolf, who was already on his feet, rifle in hand. "Goldy!" he called sharply.

The horse inquiringly turned its head. "Git out, Goldy. Git out, Goldy. Git out, Goldy!" Hatfield called in a kind of singsong voice. At the same time he held his free arm out stiffly, then swung it sharply to the right.

Long hours of patient training on Hatfield's part had taught Goldy to understand both words and pantomime. The horse understood that he was to move swiftly down the ridge and cut to the right at the first place that offered passageway. He did not need to be told that he had to avoid the approaching humans.

Goldy understood that he was to go into temporary hiding, at the same time remaining within hailing distance of his master. Experience had taught him that his master's whistle carried far and that a blast blown by strong lungs through a rifle barrel carried farther.

"At least *he'll* be safe," Hatfield muttered as he watched the horse turn at the bottom of the ridge and disappear in the rocky jumble that led to the crevasse Evans had mentioned.

"An' you'll be dead," the latter choked. "My God, Jim

Hatfield, couldn't you listen to me?"

"Hand me those glasses, Bill," Hatfield said grimly. "I want to git a good look at those whites. If I size 'em up to be varmints, I'll know what to do. Don't take it so hard. I was goin' to visit the Apaches anyway. Now that they're comin' to visit me, saves me the trip. OK, Bill, here're the glasses. Look through 'em an' watch two varmints die."

In that instant the Lone Wolf became only a pair of eyes— a pair of eyes married to a rifle that was as much a part of him as the eyes themselves. He breathed deeply. He felt the breeze against his cheek, calculating what it might do to the as yet motionless bullet when a pressure of the finger would send it speeding into the freedom of the open air. His eyes had selected their target and the muzzle of the rifle was like a third eye that kept track, unblinkingly, of the target's movements.

With held breath, he triggered.

"Got him," Bill Evans whispered hoarsely.

The words were hardly out of his mouth when the rifle spoke again. The powerful field glasses brought the result close to Bill Evans. He saw a short, dark-faced man suddenly spin completely around and come face forward again. But face, clearly discernible before, seemed all at once to be wearing a red mask. The mask, however, was made of a fluid stuff that ran and spread and dripped from his chin.

"Got 'em both," Evans breathed.

"Recognize one of 'em?" the Lone Wolf asked calmly.

"Yes," Bill said in wonder. "Pancho Juárez wanted fer murder in Coahuila. Every Ranger was told to watch out fer him an' drive him back into Mexico when found, unofficially o' course, since we had no legal power to arrest an' extradite. It was to be a matter o' courtesy to the government o' Coahuila. Reckon you done extradited him, Jim. The Apaches have taken over. I don't see a move down there.

Reckon them two messengers o' sudden death must've seemed to them like visitations from the Great Spirit hisself. They're stopped fer the time bein'."

"Good," said Hatfield, breathing deeply.

But Bill Evans's eyes were sad. His spirits had been uplifted for the moment by the marvelous accuracy of the Lone Wolf's shooting, but now, in the lull that held sway, he saw the situation as it really was, and wondered why Hatfield didn't see it.

"The Apaches will have more sense than the whites," he said. "You can't insult them into the open like I did those others. They'll know what to do an' they'll do it. They'll wait an' we'll starve. Why didn't you go when I told you to, Jim?"

"They won't wait an' we won't starve," Hatfield said, his brows furrowed with plans. "You've got to know the Indian mind, Bill. Those Apaches have been promised somethin', an' in exchange fer that promise, whatever it was, they accepted white leadership. So the first thing to do was to kill that leadership. That's been done. So the Apaches are already thinkin' . . . what kind o' leadership was that? 'The Great Spirit wasn't pleased with these white men,' they're sayin' to themselves right now. If I'd've missed both o' them, Bill, or even only one o' them, there'd've been a doubt in their minds. That's why I had to take damn' good care not to miss. You're right, Bill, we won't get 'em up here by insultin' them, but we'll get 'em up here. You jest keep them glasses lined to your eyes. If you see a hostile move, jest say my name an' I'll drop to the ground. Incidentally, do you remember the name o' their chief?"

"It's funny you shouldn't remember it, Jim," Bill said with a wry smile. "It's Shawn Loop . . . *Lone Wolf*."

Hatfield grinned. "So it is. He's down there?"

"I saw him."

"All right, Bill. Here goes."

Leaning the rifle against the wall, Hatfield went to the mouth of the cave. Then, cupping his mouth with his hands, he sent his voice roaring down the ridge.

"Shawn Loop, you have been deceived! You have been deceived by evil men! You have listened to false promises! Shawn Loop, my name, too, is Shawn Loop. So, when you listen to my voice, it will be as though you are talking to yourself. When one talks to oneself, one believes. So listen to me and believe what I say.

"I come as the servant of the Great White Father, who does not forget his promises, though he is far away. In another moment I will step out from my shelter. My hands will be bare. I will carry in them no weapon of death. I will ask only to talk to you.

"Behold, we are only two men, and you are many. So, if my talk is not good in your ears, you will still be able to lay siege to us. Nothing will be changed. But I think, if you listen to what I say, you will find my words good. Shawn Loop, I come!"

Jim went out into the open unarmed, his right hand raised and held palm outward. For an instant nothing stirred below. Fascinated, Bill peered through the glasses. The instant passed. Still nothing happened.

"I see what's wrong," Bill Evans muttered. "I've got to get up an' show myself, too . . . otherwise, they'll suspect I'm jest waitin' in here to take a pot shot."

Painfully he rose and staggered out, stumbled to Jim's side, and grasped his arm for support. Together they stood there, watching, waiting, each experiencing a queer feeling of nakedness standing there without their guns. The instant seemed to stretch out into eternity. Then both saw it at the same time—a lifted arm. That was all. For the moment only that arm, with the hand held palm outward, was visible. Then Shawn Loop himself stepped fully into view from behind a rock.

A deep sigh issued from Bill Evans's lips. "Damned if he ain't comin' up," he murmured reverently. "Alone, too."

"Which one of you calls himself by my name?"

The question was asked by the chief as he stood, lonely and defenseless, before the two white men. He, too, had played a hunch in deciding to ascend the ridge, although in his Indian tongue there was no such word as "hunch"—instead it was *tah-moss,* which meant "spirit's whisper". It was the Indian way of saying that the person hearing it should obey an inward prompting.

Shawn Loop had felt an inward prompting. It had told him to ascend the ridge and listen to these two white men so strong in warfare, especially the white man who bore the same name as he.

"I am he who is called Lone Wolf," Hatfield answered calmly. "Unlike Shawn Loop of the Apaches, I was not born with that name, it was given to me. But it is nonetheless my name. I can see that Shawn Loop has heard *tah-moss.* It is good."

The chief was startled that the white man should have read his mind so well, but only the sudden flicker of his eyelids gave evidence of his surprise.

"The Lone Wolf shoots straight," he said. "It must be the Great Spirit who directs his aim."

"The Great Spirit is always on the side of those whose cause is just," Jim said meaningly. "Shawn Loop, look upon this."

He held out his hand. In its palm something shone. It was his ranger's badge—a silver star in a silver circle. "Shawn Loop knows what it is I show him. He knows that the men who wear it never speak with a crooked tongue."

The Indian nodded.

"Shawn Loop look at this." And out of his saddlebag Jim drew the golden-haired scalp. He said nothing further, merely held it up to the chief's gaze and waited for what he had to say. It spoke louder than any words, it accused, it cried for an explanation.

It did what Hatfield had calculated it would do. Shawn Loop made no attempt to deny the raids on the ranches. He tacitly admitted them by pointing to the scalp and speaking: "This was not done by my will. The raids I admit, but no scalps were to be taken. It must have been that one of my braves, in the heat of battle, remembered the ways of his fathers."

"Why did the Apaches come out of the mountains to burn and slay?" Hatfield asked.

Shawn Loop straightened and his ordinarily stern features grew even sterner. "Why was there a treaty for the Comanches and none for the Apaches?" he responded. "Why was land to be given to the Comanches and none to the Apaches? Why were the Apaches, and not the Comanches, to be driven out of even these mountains, after they had already been driven up from the plains? Shawn Loop who is white accuses Shawn Loop who is red. Shawn Loop who is red asks for an answer to his questions."

"Why did Shawn Loop listen to lies?" Hatfield replied. "Who told him that the Apaches were to be driven away? Who told him that there was no treaty for them? Who told him that there was to be no land for them? Who kept from them the truth, which is that they were *not* to be driven out, that there was a treaty, and that my white brother who stands beside me was the bearer of that treaty?"

Shawn Loop, Indian though he was, could not suppress a start at hearing this last piece of information. For a moment he lost the power of speech. "We were told," he said, pointing at Bill, "that this one was a scout, sent out to spy upon us in preparation for the white man's attempt to drive us southward. I do not understand. I see he has made many dead, and that he remained alive. Yet, even up to today, I permitted myself to be deceived. When the white men who still remained alive came to me for help, I consented. Here I am, the white men are dead, and you tell me strange things.

"Oh, Lone Wolf, who is white, now I see that the Apaches have done wrong. Now I see that they have swallowed lies. Now I see that they were not to be driven away but were to be given land, like the Comanches, and that they did not have to do the deed that was intended to fasten guilt upon the Comanches. There was land enough for all.

"Oh, Lone Wolf, Shawn Loop has lost face. He stands before you guilty and ashamed. But his people should not be held responsible for the evil they have done. Shawn Loop is their chief. The guilt is his alone, for believing crooked tongues, for allowing his heart to grow bitter over what was not true. Shawn Loop will take his people's sin upon himself.

"Shawn Loop is prepared to have the white man wreak justice upon him. Shawn Loop is prepared to die. But Shawn Loop asks only one favor. Shawn Loop does not want the rope around his neck. He does not want to dance upon the air. Let Shawn Loop die by his own hand, let him plunge his own dagger into his breast."

With the last words Shawn Loop drew his knife.

"Put back your knife, Shawn Loop," Hatfield said.

The chief hesitated.

"Put back your knife," Hatfield repeated sharply. "Neither I nor the Great White Father desire your death. The evil that has been done is not the work of the Apaches, but of those who led the Apaches on to do it. It is they who must be punished. Had my brother been permitted to come to you with the treaty, none of the evil would have happened. He was not permitted to come. Who stopped him? Who told the Apaches lies? Give me the name of the man."

"He who was called Wah-rezz," the Apache chief answered.

"Juárez, yes," Hatfield said. "Juárez is dead, but it was not his brain that spun the plan. Who was behind Juárez? That is what I want to know. Can Shawn Loop tell me?"

The chief shook his head. "I only know, that he for whom Wah-rezz acted was called by him the King of the Angels. Juárez spoke of a man who had it in his power to give to the Apaches all the land that once had been theirs."

"Angels," Hatfield murmured to himself. "Devils would be more like it. But angels . . . that means something." He turned to Bill Evans. "This business looks more an' more like it's got two parts to it," he said. "One's shore enough Mexican and the other's Texan. King of the Angels. Coahuila in Mexico. The Angela Mesa in Texas. Well, Bill," Hatfield said smiling, "we've found a way to get you the rest an' care you need. You're goin' with Shawn Loop. You're goin' to negotiate that treaty with him, after all. Here it is. An' you'll rest up in Shawn Loop's lodge until you're fit to travel back to the station. I told you, Bill, that you weren't goin' to die, an' you ain't. You were afraid you were in my way. Well, you ain't. I'm free to act again, an' the first thing I'd better do, I'm thinkin', is to investigate the presence of those Mexicans on Texas soil . . . you were tellin' me about."

Hatfield watched Bill Evans's face for signs of recollection and was prepared to see none. But Evans face lit up with the memory.

"Yep, I reckon that's what you'd better do," Bill Evans said earnestly.

Hatfield's face became grave. He had hoped, in fact he had been all but certain that those Mexicans had existed only in the injured Ranger's imagination. But now he was no longer sure, one way or the other. It meant further delay for he would have to investigate.

The Lone Wolf whistled shrilly. After an instant's silence a distant whinny came in reply. Soon they heard the beat of hoofs. The golden horse seemed to appear out of nowhere. Half an hour later, his mind at rest concerning Bill Evans, the Lone Wolf was riding again.

IX

Jim Hatfield rode for the remainder of that morning and well into the afternoon, yet the downward-dipping sun found him still in the inhospitable fastnesses of the Chisos Mountains. They were like a labyrinth. The trails seemed to lead to nowhere, and the valleys into which he descended, instead of rolling out onto the plain, came to a dead end against unscalable cliffs.

Yet there had to be a route through the Chisos Mountains, he reasoned, else the party of horsemen Evans had mentioned would have been visible on the prairie to the east when he had looked for them. Unless—and the thought still troubled him—there was no party of horsemen at all. Unless they had merely been the product of Bill's fevered imagination.

If that's so, he thought, *I'm wastin' time. I ain't seen a trail sign or heard a human sound ever since I left Bill. Mebbe he was jest seein' things.* "Goldy, we'll try that hump over there. If there's nothing on the other side, we'll git out of here."

Half an hour later, halting on the crest, he chuckled. "Here she be." Looking to the south, he saw how the trail snaked up and into the mountains.

"This is it," he muttered. "If there ever was a party o' horsemen, this is where they'll come out. Chisos, you shore had me buffaloed fer a while. But here I am, an' there's the prairie so close that I could almost spit down on it. I shore am surprised. Goldy, I reckon we'll jest mosey down there an' wait a spell."

He descended and took up a position on a knoll that had some grass for Goldy to crop. The patient horse allayed its hunger, then looked, like its master, southward. There was something strangely impressive in the sight of that horse and rider standing, lonely and motionless, there.

"Goldy," Hatfield muttered, "if Bill wasn't mistaken about what he says he saw, an' I ain't mistaken about what I think it means, then you an' me are where we ought to be, gittin' ready once more to stop somethin' before it starts."

He felt the horse suddenly quiver beneath him. He knew what that meant—Goldy had heard something. Another horse would have responded with a nicker, but Goldy had been trained against making sounds that might spell danger for his master. Hatfield, looking through his field glasses, at first saw nothing, but a minute later he was thankful for Goldy's warning.

"Horse, you shore got ears," he muttered. Hatfield felt a tremor go up and down Goldy's spine. The Lone Wolf sat motionlessly as he watched a column of horsemen, still far away, advance down the trail. The column seemed endless. Bill Evans's estimate had fallen far short of their actual number; Jim calculated that there were close to 800 men in the party. They were Mexicans—all armed—and on Texas soil!

He continued to look through the glasses. His eyes suddenly sharpened in disbelief.

" 'Tain't possible," he muttered. "Why, that *hombre* ridin' up front . . . he's. . . ."

No, it wasn't possible. The face of the man who rode in the van of the oncoming troop was the same as the face he had seen. . . . No, it couldn't be. That other man, when he had seen him, had been dead in Devil's Pass, with his hand clasping another's.

Jim Hatfield was dazed, but only for an instant. Then the only possible explanation came to him—this man he was seeing now was not a dead man returned to life, but he was that dead man's brother, perhaps even his twin. He was an Alvarez. There could no longer be any doubt that his presence on Texas soil was tied up with the Devil's Pass tragedy.

Meanwhile, the sight of Jim Hatfield was having its effect on the troop. It had slowed down and was advancing toward him at a walk. In truth there was something mysterious, even awe-inspiring, about that motionless horse and rider.

"He is a Texan," the man riding next to the leader said, unconsciously lowering his voice to a whisper, "a *gringo,* the first we have seen since crossing the river. Let us begin our vengeance now. Give me the word, *Don* Pedro, and I will shoot."

A spasm of bitterness contorted the leader's face. He seemed on the point of giving the word his companion asked for. A struggle seemed to take place within him. Then he shook his head.

"No," he said, "not yet. He is one man and we are many hundreds. He stands there waiting, and he seems to be waiting for us. His rifle is slung, and his hands are away from his guns. He has seen us through field glasses, has seen that we are Mexicans, nevertheless he has not fled. Should he turn to flee, then shoot. But, otherwise, we must first learn who he is, and why he waits there."

Perhaps Hatfield sensed what was being discussed for he said to Goldy: "I'm a-thinkin' my life ain't worth a damn if those *hombres* are of a mind to shoot first an' ask questions after. But what kin we do, sorrel horse, we got ourselves into this an' we'll have to stick it out. If we made a break fer it, we'd shore be riddled."

Slowly, as the troop drew nearer, he raised his hand. The

gesture was one of peace, but it was also one of authority.

The men in the van of the troop drew rein in front of Hatfield and the Ranger fastened his eyes on the leader. Then slowly he lowered his hand, held it out, and spoke softly in Spanish.

"*Señor* Alvarez," he said, "take my hand."

An expression of amazement, both at Hatfield's knowledge of his name and at the strange request, spread over the leader's handsome face.

"Who are you?" he demanded. "How do you know my name? Above all, what are you doing here?"

"*Señor* Alvarez, take my hand," the Lone Wolf repeated, and there was something in his tones so compelling, so urgent, that the leader found himself obeying the request in spite of himself. Once the hand was in his own, Hatfield did not let go of it, but continued to speak as though he wanted the seriousness of his words to be communicated to the other by touch as well as by sound. "*Señor* Alvarez, there must be no war between Mexicans and Texans. I hold your hand in mine so that, when you speak and promise me that there will not be war, your words will be an oath and a promise that cannot be broken."

The amazement deepened in the Mexican's eyes. "What manner of man are you?" he asked in wonder. "You speak as though with the knowledge of things unknown to me. Explain yourself and your presence here."

"Not until *Señor* Alvarez confesses with his own lips that his presence and the presence of his men on Texas soil means war," Jim Hatfield answered.

"I will not speak until you tell me how you know me," the Mexican replied.

"*Señor*," the Lone Wolf said calmly, "you resemble your brother."

"And you knew my brother?" the Mexican asked.

"You say *knew, señor* . . . not know. That tells me that you know your brother is dead. That is why you are here, *señor,* is it not? You do not need to tell me. I will tell you."

Then the Ranger, still holding the Mexican's hand in his, proceeded to tell him why he had come into Texas—to avenge his brother's death and the death of all the others, because he believed that Texans were responsible for it. The Mexican listened, his handsome face growing more and more contorted.

"Yes," he said in a choked voice, when Jim had finished, "that is why we are here. It costs me nothing to tell you so, for I can have you shot down like a dog, and the information will die with you. I think you are a madman, *señor.* Otherwise, you would not have risked falling into our hands . . . you, a Texan, after what Texans have done! And you have the mad audacity to sit there and calmly tell it to me, the brother . . . the twin brother of the dead man?"

"I have not said that Texans did it," Jim said. "I have not finished speaking. So far I have only told you what you *believe* to be so. I have not yet told you what *is* so. But before I do, I must ask you to tell me how you learned of the massacre in Devil's Pass. I have reasons for knowing that, *señor,* for I believe that your presence on Texas soil, away from Coahuila, may not be displeasing to a certain party, or parties, still unknown to me." Hatfield paused for a minute. "Speak, *Señor* Alvarez. As you say, anything you tell me will cost you nothing, for you can always shoot me."

"There was a survivor of the massacre," *Don* Pedro said in a low voice. "He came back to Coahuila with the tale of what had happened."

"Does he happen to be with you now?" the Ranger asked.

"Sanchez! Come forward!" *Don* Pedro cried.

A Mexican rode out from the mass of men. "Tell us what happened, Sanchez," Hatfield said, eyeing him keenly.

The Mexican turned to *Don* Pedro. "I have told the story a dozen times," he said sullenly. "Is it necessary for me to tell it to a stranger?"

"Never mind, Sanchez," the Ranger said sharply. "Instead of listening to you, I will ask *Señor* Alvarez another question. Are you able to state positively that Sanchez was a member of your brother's party?"

Jim Hatfield's next move was lightning-like. It had to be. Even as he had asked the question, he had been prepared for Sanchez's reaction. Dropping Alvarez's hand, one prod from his spurs was sufficient to send Goldy ranging alongside the Mexican. The Ranger's arm shot out and his fingers closed in a steely grip about the Mexican's wrist. Sanchez had drawn his gun half out of its holster.

"Don't shoot, anybody!" Hatfield shouted at the same time. "I am not going to harm this man!" He kept tight hold of the Mexican's wrist. "You have all seen," he said. "Sanchez was going to shoot me."

"Why not!" the Mexican blazed. "Did you not all hear the *gringo* call me a liar?"

"I did not call you a liar," Hatfield said. "I simply asked *Señor* Alvarez whether or not he knew positively that *you* were a member of his brother's party."

"Give me your gun, Sanchez," *Don* Pedro said quietly. "I will answer your question, *señor*. I cannot tell you of my own knowledge whether or not Sanchez was a member. The men were recruited from the different villages. My brother attended to all that. But why do you ask the question, *señor*? What reason have you for doubting the presence of Sanchez?"

The piercing eyes of the Lone Wolf found those of Sanchez.

"No man could have escaped death in Devil's Pass that day," Hatfield said. "Since that is so, then Sanchez could not have been a member of your brother's party. If he had been a member, he would be dead. But he's alive, as you all can see. Sanchez has been the instrument to drag you and your men into Texas and into war, *Señor* Alvarez. Sanchez did not survive any massacre, because he was never in any massacre. He may have seen the massacre, but, if he did, it was from a point of safety. If he had told you the truth, he would have told you that in order to get out of Devil's Pass he would have had to run the gauntlet through a party of men who had nothing to do with either your brother's expedition or John Holcomb's . . . he would have had to escape the real murderers.

"But," Hatfield continued, looking at the cringing Sanchez, "he has told you nothing of such men. That is why I knew he was lying. For I myself had to break through such a cordon at the northern end of the pass, and there was enough evidence to show me that the same would have been true at the southern end. The time has come for me to tell you, *Señor* Alvarez, that your brother, *Don* José, died with his hand in the hand of John Holcomb. The time has come for me to tell you what you first asked me, who I am. I am Jim Hatfield, Texas Ranger. The time has come that you should be shown the last will and testament of José Alvarez and John Holcomb. Here it is."

The blood left *Don* Pedro's face as he read the bloody message of the shirt. When he had finished, and before Hatfield could stop him, he drew his gun and shot Sanchez dead.

"He was a dog," he murmured, terrible-eyed. "He deserved to die like one. *Señor,* I am dazed. What you have said to me and shown me is almost more than my mind can bear. I shudder now to think what might have happened had you not been here, waiting. You have prevented further massacres.

You have stopped me from doing a great and terrible wrong."

"I'm sorry I couldn't have stopped you from shooting that man as well," Hatfield answered soberly.

"Why, *señor?*"

"We might have learned something from him. Dead men tell no tales." He shook his head ruefully. "I suppose I'm not the one to talk," he continued. "Ever since I've been on this case, I've been making corpses of men who might otherwise have furnished me with the information I needed. But in this case it might have been better if you had waited. Perhaps we would have learned who the man is who is called El Rey de Angeles."

Don Pedro gave a start. "What name did you just speak?" he asked in tones of amazement.

"El Rey de Angeles," Hatfield repeated, his voice vibrant. Was it possible that he was about to learn something definite at last?

"Jaime Galdos y Cabrera was called the King of the Angels," *Don* Pedro said slowly.

"Who is Jaime Galdos y Cabrera?" Hatfield asked, a deep furrow between his eyes.

Don Pedro shook his head like a man dazed. "Jaime Galdos y Cabrera has been dead forty years," he said.

The information was like a dash of cold water over the Lone Wolf's hopes. "Dead men don't commit raids and massacres," he said dryly.

"But he had sons, *señor,*" *Don* Pedro said in a low voice.

Hatfield pricked up his ears.

"The Cabreras have been enemies of my family for generations," the *don* went on. "But they have been out of power since Jaime Galdos died. At the time of the Texas war for independence, he was ruler over Coahuila. He ruled with an iron hand, like an absolute monarch, and his kingdom comprised no only the great district of Coahuila but extended into Texas as well. The very land we are now on was his. Even the rich range lands of the Great Angela Mesa belonged to him and his sister. The sister married an American, but her heart, I am told, remained in Mexico. For many years she dreamed of the revolution that would win back Coahuila for the Cabreras . . . what is it? You look at me so strangely."

"Nothing," said the Lone Wolf. "Go on."

But to himself he was thinking excitedly: *It all ties in. The Great Angela Mesa . . . once it was Mexican, once it belonged to the Cabreras. And the last of the Cabreras, the present generation, want it back.* His thoughts hesitated, stumbled. *But could Mexicans, the sons of old Cabrera . . . could they come into Texas an' do what's already been done . . . the massacre in Devil's Pass, the enlistment of the Apaches, the raids on the mesa, the stopping of Bill . . . could they have done all that alone? No*—Hatfield's thoughts hurried on—*this business isn't all Mexican. It's part Texan. Those varmints in the Lone Star Saloon . . . only one of them was Mexican. No, this business is part Texan. Someone in Texas has a hand in it. Maybe it's a small hand, maybe a big hand, but it's someone who could plan ahead and who could arrange to time things so that they'd take place when he wanted them to take place.* Hatfield was remembering the massacre, the raids. *There's a single force at work, but it's in two parts. There's Mexican politics mixed up in this, or I miss my guess. Here are all these men, away from home. Why? Because someone wants them here. Old Cabrera had a sister. I'll have to question the* don *further about that. She married an American. If she had children. . . .*

The Ranger broke off his thoughts suddenly as he noticed the *don* waiting for him to give him his attention. "Pardon me," he said. "My thoughts have wandered."

"You seemed like a man wrapped in the spell of some dream," the *don* said. "To continue. At the time your people

151

won their independence, my family wrested power from the Cabreras. Ever since then the people of Coahuila have been free, for we divided the land up among them. Their only enemies since that time have been drought and famine, for people cannot eat silver. That is why my brother and John Holcomb arranged that exchange which ended so tragically."

"What became of the sons of the Cabrera family?" Hatfield asked, his eyes narrowed.

"The Cabrera family dispersed into Chihuahua. When the sons grew up, they degenerated into bandits."

"Where are they now?"

"One was killed in a raid, one of many, which he attempted on a Coahuila village. The other still lives. Perhaps it is he who has taken his father's name . . . the King of the Angels. Only, if that is so, he is a king without a kingdom, a king in exile."

"I've heard that kings in exile try to get back their kingdoms," the Ranger said meaningfully. "Alvarez, don't you begin to see the purpose behind all this? Don't you see that someone had a reason for drawing you and all these men up into Texas, away from home?"

The color seemed to leave the *don*'s face. "Yes," he breathed almost to himself. "Yes. I begin to see now. I have blundered. What am I to do? Perhaps you, who are so wise, can tell me. The silver is gone, the cattle that were exchanged for it and that my people needed with such a great need are also gone. And now you have made me see that there is danger at home, because I have withdrawn so many men who would be needed in a defense against any attack. . . ."

"This is what you must do, *Señor* Alvarez," Hatfield said, speaking decisively. "You must send your men back . . . at once. You must send a message back with them, to your brother, the governor, telling him what you suspect."

"And I? You speak as though I should not go with them."

"No. Your work is here, in Texas. Since Coahuila needs cattle so badly, you must negotiate for them in Texas. What good would defending Coahuila do, unless you can make Coahuila worth defending? Coahuila needs cattle. You must get them."

"But the silver is gone . . . ," said *Don* Pedro dejectedly.

"I'll find the silver," snapped Hatfield.

"But why are you, a Texan, doing so much for a people who are not your own?" *Don* Pedro asked in amazement tinged with a great respect.

"*Señor* Alvarez," Hatfield said slowly, "you should not have to ask me that. I took the bloody shirt from the dead hand of your brother. From the moment I did that and read what was on it, I became the man who had to do what the blood of your brother and John Holcomb demanded that I do. That blood will not take no for an answer. They said . . . 'We leave this record, so that our deaths may be avenged.' The record fell into my hands. I have no choice but to do what it says. But there are other reasons. I'm working for Texas, too. And Coahuila governed by the Alvarezes is all right with Texas. But Coahuila governed by bandits *isn't* all right. Don't you see? All this business is mixed up together. Massacres, raids, attempts on my life, and the life of another Ranger. I'll tell you about that when we get under way."

"But where are we going?"

"To the Angela Mesa, to the great ranch of a man who must be wondering whether I'm his hired hand or not . . . to Sam Morgan. He'll sell you cattle, unless I've very much mistaken. And, besides, it's time I was back there. There must be plenty of Comanche braves, very good friends of mine, who are getting mighty tired of hiding behind women and children, not to mention the women who would rather be doing their woman's work and the children who would rather be playing. Will you go with me, *Señor* Alvarez?"

"Jim Hatfield," *Don* Pedro said slowly, "I think I would go with you wherever you asked."

"Listen!" Hatfield said suddenly.

Through the air came the hoof beats and the snorting of a horse. As if by magic a mounted figure appeared on the crest of the hill over which Hatfield had come when he had about given up the belief that Bill Evans had really seen the Mexicans. The mounted figure stood for an instant as though frozen, a statue with hand upraised, palm outward.

It was Shawn Loop, the chief of the Apaches.

X

Suddenly the statue came to life. In another minute the chief was facing Hatfield.

"How," Shawn Loop said in greeting.

"How," Jim Hatfield answered. "What brings you here?" His voice was tense with anxiety. "Is it Evans? Is he worse? Is he . . . ?"

"Your friend is well. He sent me to find you. It was like searching for the ghost of a wolf, but Shawn Loop was taught to trail almost before he could walk. Here I am, with news that your Ranger brother said you had to have."

"What is it?" Hatfield asked urgently.

"After you left, your friend decided to rest before coming to my lodge. He was tired. I waited with him. With the thing that makes the eye see far into the distance, he looked to the south. There he saw men, many men. He gave me the thing to look through. I too saw men, many men. But they were not white men, but Indians . . . Yaquis."

"What were they doing?"

For answer Shawn Loop dismounted, motioning for Hatfield to do likewise. With the point of his knife—the same knife that not many hours before he had been about to plunge into his breast—he drew a map on the ground. *Don* Pedro dismounted. The two knelt while the Indian completed the map. When he had finished, the *don* turned to Hatfield. "What does it mean?" he asked.

"It's plain," the Ranger said. "A force of men have taken

up a position which seems designed to stop any retreat from this side of the Chisos Mountains. That means you, Alvarez . . . you and your force. El Rey de Angeles, or whoever is behind this black business, is devilishly smart, he plans ahead."

Hatfield looked at the crude map that Shawn Loop had drawn. He examined the spots that indicated men.

"That devil not only drew you up into Texas, but he's taken steps to keep you here, to prevent your getting back into Coahuila. That was in case anything went wrong with his plan up to that point. Well, you see that something did go wrong . . . you met me. And you *were* about to send your men home."

"Then we stay here," *Don* Pedro said decisively. "We will not play into this unknown man's game by running into an ambush. We stay in Texas."

"You'll do nothing of the kind," Hatfield said. "You say you don't want to play into his hands. What do you suppose you'd be doing if you remained in Texas? A large party of armed Mexicans on Texas soil means trouble. Trouble is what he, whoever he is, wants. If he couldn't get it between Comanches and Texans, he planned to get it between Mexicans and Texans. That's why you're here. And now because he wanted you *in,* you've got to get out! The only way out is through. Shawn Loop here has a seeing eye. His map tells us all we need to know. We're not going to run into any ambush. We're going to attack!"

The *don* seemed to take fire at these words. "Yes!" he exclaimed. "Yes, you are right!" He called out to his men: "You are to take orders from *Señor* Hatfield! From this minute forward, he is in command! Rubio! Rodriguez! Vega! Come forward. These are my lieutenants, *señor*."

Hatfield was studying the map as the men came forward.

"Good," he muttered. Then he spoke aloud. "Shawn Loop, you have much to make up for. Here is your chance to do so. Will you and your braves fight on the side of the white man?"

"Shawn Loop was prepared to do so without being asked," the Indian replied gravely.

"Good. Then you must return to your village at once and gather your braves together. You will then move south in a wide curve so as to come up behind the Yaquis . . . here." He pointed to a position on the map.

The chest of the Indian swelled at prospect of battle. Without another word he mounted, raised his hand high in farewell, and rode off.

"Can we depend on him?" the *don* asked almost nervously.

"Without a doubt," the Lone Wolf answered. "There won't be any retreat for those Yaquis if we time it right. I suppose they've got scouts out, so they'll know a part of what we're doing. But they won't know about the Apaches. We're going to move forward. When we reach this point here"—he pointed out the spot on the map—"we're going to split off half our men for a flanking attack. But we'll split them off a few at a time, so the movement won't be noticed. The rest of us will drive forward."

"But what about the eastern flank?"

"See this?" Hatfield said. "That's the Indian sign for a chasm. That chasm makes a fourth division unnecessary." Hatfield looked up at the sun. "I figure we'll have two hours of daylight from the time the battle begins," he said. "That'll be enough time to do a good job of fighting, or dying, as the case may be."

The face of the *don* was troubled. "But you," he said, "you who have so much to do, here in Texas, you whose life is so important to your people, need you risk it in this adventure? Will it not be enough if I go with my men, now that you have told me what is to be done?"

"It wasn't you who found your brother's shirt," the Ranger answered softly. "I did."

The *don* was silent. There was nothing more to be said.

800 men, who did not know whether they would ever come out, moved into the Chisos Mountains. For a time those 800 men were a single force. Then gradually, under Hatfield's skillful direction, their numbers lessened. Singly, in twos, or threes, they dropped away from the rear of the troop and seemed to fade into the hills on their right.

Each man had the same orders—to move west for about a mile, then south, and finally to come together where Shawn Loop had indicated the presence of pine woods. This would bring them down on the left flank of the Yaquis.

The 800 men became 700, then 600, finally 400. But spreading out under the Ranger's orders, there seemed to be as large a number as before—at least to a distant observer, if there happened to be one.

Meanwhile, if the Lone Wolf's faith in the Indian were not misplaced, Shawn Loop and his warriors were ghosting south in a wide arc that would bring them around behind the enemy. The afternoon sun moved down the sky. The mountain breeze freshened.

Soon there'll be the smell of gunfire to spoil it, thought Hatfield. "Listen!" he said to *Don* Pedro as the howl of a coyote came from up ahead. "I figure that came from where Shawn Loop indicated there were woods."

"Is that important?" the *don* asked.

"Yes," Hatfield muttered, "because that sound wasn't made by a coyote . . . it came from a human throat. Hear that? It's being answered from over on the right. They're waiting for us, and they're telling each other that we're coming. But two can play at that game. We'll know in a short while whether or not Shawn Loop is on the job."

"How are you going to know that?"

Hatfield looked up at the sun once more. "I reckon Shawn Loop has had enough time," he muttered. "Listen."

Don Pedro listened. Suddenly he was almost startled out of his skin. From beside him, without warning, rose the long, mournful, far-carrying howl of a wolf. If *Don* Pedro had not known better, he would have thought that a wolf had come up under the very hoofs of his horse. But it was the throat of Jim Hatfield that gave vent to that sound. The wolf that made it was human and lonely—the white Shawn Loop, the Lone Wolf of the Texas Rangers.

"The Apaches use the cry of a wolf as a signal," Hatfield said to the startled *don*, who was having trouble controlling his frightened horse. "If Shawn Loop's hearing is as keen as I think it is, he won't make the same mistake as your horse. He'll know that howl was human and that it was intended as a signal. He's probably heard the coyote howls and figured what they were, so he'll know the wolf howl came from us."

"But it sounded so much like a wolf," the *don* said. "How will the Apache know otherwise? And if he does know otherwise, why won't the Yaquis also know?"

"Shawn Loop will answer, whether he knows positively it was a signal or not. He'll take a chance that it was. The Yaquis won't have the same reason for thinking it was a signal as he, so the chances are they'll think it was just a wolf. Listen!"

The *don* felt his scalp prickle, as though the hair was rising on his head. A shiver ran up and down his spine. He heard it. It came from the south and from a distance, but it was unmistakable. Somewhere to the south a wolf was answering the Ranger's call, and, if that wolf was human, it meant that Shawn Loop and his warriors had come up behind the enemy.

Once again the eerie sound welled from Hatfield's throat. This was to tell Shawn Loop that his answer had been heard and understood. Then the troop moved onward, entering the wooded growth that marked the beginning of the mountain forest that had appeared on Shawn Loop's map.

Hatfield gave the order for the troop to spread out fanwise, with its flanks curving forward so that the formation was like an inverted arc. Each man, however, was to do his best to keep in touch with the men nearest him. The Ranger gave the order to dismount at the first sound of gunfire. The horses, all bridle wise, were to be left untethered in the rear.

It was dark and chill in the woods. The trees shut out the sunlight. The spot was so quiet, so peaceful, that it was difficult to believe that somewhere up ahead, in the woods and back of them, a human barrier waited, blocking the way to Mexico.

"Rubio ought to be in position by now," Jim Hatfield said in a low voice.

It had been pre-arranged that Lieutenant Rubio was to fire three shots as soon as he got into flanking position and judged that there had been enough time for Shawn Loop to execute his maneuver. Jim had purposely kept down the speed of his own force in order to bring the three separate bodies into action at as nearly the same time as possible.

However, there was one difficulty. Although Jim had had a means of communication with Shawn Loop, he had none with the forces of Lieutenant Rubio. He now saw that this had been a mistake, and blamed himself for not thinking of the wolf call before the forces had split up. Then all three forces would have known the whereabouts of each other. As it was, Lieutenant Rubio would have to depend on dead reckoning.

Suddenly, in rapid fire, the three shots came.

"Dismount and move in!" Hatfield ordered. The command was relayed from mouth to mouth. 400 men, spread out fanwise, moved forward in the woods. Up ahead fire began to spurt.

"Fire at anything that moves!" Hatfield roared. "Fire at the flashes!" His own guns were out and he was throwing lead even as he shouted. "Why in hell is Rubio holding his fire!" he stormed, addressing the question to no one in particular.

The next instant, almost as though Lieutenant Rubio had heard him, the forest up ahead and to the right blazed with a volley from Rubio's men.

"That's more like it," Jim muttered. "Not too fast there. Keep your line and keep it curved. We're going to pinch 'em."

Swiftly he moved up the line to his right, giving orders as he went. The men on the right wing were to keep the arc unbroken and meet up with Rubio's forces. The men in the center were to hold back a little, advancing slowly in three ranks. Each man was to make use of such shelter as offered itself but to maintain a steady forward movement at the same time.

It was impossible, Hatfield saw, that such orders could be carried out to the letter, but the men were to do the best they could. Satisfied that his orders were understood, he moved back to the center. A sudden exclamation came from him.

"Sharpshooter up in a tree," he muttered. His gun barrel pointed upward, bucked in his hand. A long death wail shuddered through the tumult. There was a sound of ripping boughs as a dusky figure came tumbling through the branches of a tree not more than twenty paces ahead.

"*Bueno*," a voice beside Hatfield said. It was *Don* Pedro, sweating and disheveled, his rifle hot in his hands. "Why haven't your Indians opened fire yet?" the *don* demanded.

"I was thinking of that," Jim Hatfield answered quickly. "It may be that Shawn Loop figures that his fire would drive the Yaquis back onto us, and that wouldn't be so good for us. He's waiting for us to drive the Yaquis back to him. Shawn Loop's intentions may be good. . . . Wait a minute! Shawn Loop's right! The chasm!"

Jim Hatfield's heart and brain were suddenly on fire with a great restlessness. It was time to make an end of this; it was time to get somewhere. Ever since he had been on this Devil's Pass job—that's what he called it—he had been delayed and delayed.

First it had been the death of Ned Markham, necessitating the trip to the Carson Ranger station. Then it had been the siege of Bill Evans. Now it was *Don* Pedro and the fate of Coahuila. It was true that it had been absolutely necessary to take these into account, to stop an Indian war, to stop a war between Texans and Mexicans before it started. But the guilty party, the man behind all this—who was he, where was he?

It was that thought that was burning in Hatfield's brain; it was that thought that made him anxious to return to the Angela Mesa. For he was absolutely certain that the Devil's Pass massacre and all that went with it was not one-sided—it was not all Mexican. He was certain that it had its roots in Texas, too. Otherwise, why should there have been those Indian raids on Texas ranches? If the thing was Mexican alone, why had it not been enough merely to draw *Don* Pedro and the pick of his fighting men out of Coahuila?

"We're going up!" Hatfield snapped to the *don*. "We're going to finish this and finish it quick. Move down the line and tell the men to advance firing with everything they've got as soon as they hear my shout. I'll take care of the left wing. It may mean hand-to-hand fighting, but in that case they can use their gun butts and knives, and if necessary their bare hands. If our charge is fierce enough, we can drive them back onto Shawn Loop, who'll do the rest. Understand?"

"*Si.*"

They separated. The Lone Wolf moved off to the left, giving orders to each man as he met him, drawing them closer together where needed, spreading them where they had been bunched too closely. The two wings of the arc were curling farther inward, for the arena of action had narrowed with the changing formation of the terrain, the woods on the left thinning out and merging into rock formations that testified to the nearness of the chasm Shawn Loop had marked.

Hatfield moved back to the center, where the woods were thickest. He was confident now that some of the Yaquis were far enough forward to be well within the curve of the arc.

"Forward!" he roared out, and, deserting his shelter behind a tree, he dashed ahead to lead the rest.

From the very instant of that charge, the character of the battle changed, and the men lost contact with each other. It was every man for himself. Yet, their formation broken, they were all united in their one objective—to let nothing live that came in their way.

An irregular but vicious hail of fire and lead met their charge, but did not break it. Dusky shapes became visible men, then will-o'-the-wisp shadows, as the fire flashes came and went. Curses and cries of pain and an occasional rattle of death kept pace with the charge. Men fell with their faces forward, while the others moved on. Underneath these sounds came an occasional *twang* and a *whirr*—some of the Yaquis were using arrows.

The Lone Wolf, his dash taking him into the lead at the center, found that he had suddenly flushed two Yaquis in the process of reloading their rifles. Their sudden appearance was as much a surprise to him as his coming was to them. They dropped their rifles and flashed into action with their tomahawks.

Hatfield ducked and threw lead at the same time. The savage weapons buried themselves in the ground behind him. One of the Yaquis went down with the Ranger's bullet in his belly. The other came to physical grips with him. Hatfield jerked his right arm free of the embrace and smashed the Yaqui's skull with his gun barrel. Moving to the right, he again made contact with *Don* Pedro. The *don* had an arrow in a bicep.

"Never mind it," he panted hoarsely. "There is no time for surgery now."

"How's it going?" Hatfield asked quickly.

"So far as I have been able to see, not a single Yaqui has broken through us."

"We're almost out of the woods," Hatfield observed, and the fact was true in a figurative as well as a literal sense. "In another minute we can expect to hear from Shawn Loop. I'm going to see that the right wing. . . ."

His words were suddenly cut off by a burst of fire from up ahead. The Ranger's words had come true—it was Shawn Loop, and it meant that the Yaquis had been driven out of the woods. Jim dashed to the right. With breathtaking abruptness he found himself out in the clear.

That movement almost cost him his life. He had all but come within the line of fire of Rubio's men. He flung himself flat and turned around. There was the chasm Shawn Loop had marked on the map. And on the flat broad table of rock running down to its edge were the Yaquis. It was an indescribable scene of demoralization and panic. The retreat of the Yaquis to the south was cut off by Shawn Loop. Their way to the north was barred by *Don* Pedro. Any escape to the west was effectively blocked by the raking and merciless fire of Rubio and his men.

There remained but one means of escape—the chasm, for Hatfield's plan of battle had been carried out to the letter. Raked by a withering fire from three directions, the desperate Yaquis chanced the sheer drop to the chasm's bottom. Their bodies plummeted over the edge of the chasm that became their death crypt. The battle was decisively over.

Hatfield issued orders. Some of the men were to go back and bring up the horses. Others were to bring out the dead and give first-aid to the wounded.

"Well done," he said to Shawn Loop who had by this time joined him, and he laid his hand for an instant on the Indian's shoulder. The Indian replied with the same gesture. Hatfield stooped and picked up a rifle from the side of a dead Yaqui. He examined it curiously.

It was a weapon of a type he had never seen before. He saw at once that it was a powerful thing that could send a bullet on a far flight. Breaking it, he took out one of the cartridges. An exclamation escaped him. He extracted two bullets from his pocket, the one that had killed Ned Markham and the other that had wounded him. Hatfield compared the three. They were similar. Further investigation disclosed that several of the other Yaquis had possessed the same type of rifle. In each case the Yaqui had been a chief or sub-chief, judging from the design on his war paint.

"Who gave 'em these guns?" the Ranger wondered. "Where did they come from? Who paid fer 'em?"

"*Señor* Hatfield!" he heard the voice of *Don* Pedro calling to him. "Quick! Come here! I have something to show you!"

Hatfield went to him. The *don* pointed to a corpse.

"A white man," the Ranger muttered. "The leader, I suppose."

The *don*'s face was pale and in his eyes was an expression of disbelief. "It is even stranger than that," he said. "I can hardly believe it yet. This man is a Cabrera. More startling still he is the Cabrera who I thought had been hanged. I cannot understand it, unless the man who was hanged was mistaken for Guzman Cabrera."

"That's what probably happened," said Jim Hatfield. "Anyway, he's dead now." He was still more interested in the rifle than in the dead man. He blew a blast through the barrel, knowing that the sound would carry to Goldy and that Goldy would come. It would be good to have Goldy with him again.

Suddenly Hatfield remembered the arrow in *Don* Pedro's arm. But it had been removed and the arm was bandaged.

"Rubio took care of it," the *don* said, noticing the direction of the Ranger's gaze.

"I reckon it won't hurt to search this varmint," Hatfield muttered.

A search revealed nothing but a bag of silver, but Hatfield looked once again at the dead man's face. His gaze grew troubled. He looked more intently. That face—was it possible that he had seen it somewhere before?

He tried to dismiss the thought, knowing that it could not be true, but it persisted. It was as though someone were knocking faintly on the door of his brain, demanding admittance.

"What is it, Hatfield?" the *don* asked, struck by the faraway look in the Ranger's eyes and involuntarily lowering his voice.

"I don't know," he murmured. "I don't know."

"The Cabreras were fated to live by the sword and to die by it," the *don* said gravely. "A handsome, degenerate race without moral principles, without honor."

"Handsome," Hatfield muttered in agreement.

Again something seemed to knock on the door of his brain; he tried to open that door, but it remained shut. Somewhere he had seen that proud, handsome face. Impatience seized him once more.

"Something, I don't know what it is," he murmured, "seems to be calling me back to the Angela Mesa." His lips twisted in a faint mirthless smile. "Maybe it's the angels," he said. "The angels that gave the mesa its name. Maybe it's the king of the angels."

XI

The sun went down, the stars came out. Two lonely riders, keeping close together, left the shadow of the Chisos Mountains behind them.

"We'll bed down on the plain," Hatfield said to *Don* Pedro, "but only fer a couple of hours. I know you're tired an' could use a full night's sleep."

"And you? Are you not tired, too?"

"Reckon I'm too restless to feel tired. That isn't it, though. I'd be in favor of a full night's sleep fer the both of us, only there's a stop I want to make before goin' on to the Circle Seven. That'll take a little time."

"Where are we to make this stop?"

"Outside of Del Río. There's a man I want to see there by the name o' Hank Wilkins. I want him to do a favor fer me. I did one fer him once. You'll see what it is when we get there. Meantime, let's light an' grab what little sleep we kin."

Hatfield found sleep slow in coming. Evidently the *don* did, too, for he heard the Mexican stirring restlessly.

No use wastin' this wakefulness, he thought. Aloud he said: "You say that old Cabrera had a sister. What became of her?"

The *don* turned toward him, apparently relieved that he was not alone in his wakefulness. The lonely immensity of the plain, the stars flickering high overhead, the howl of a coyote in the distance, had given him a lost feeling, and he was glad that Hatfield was with him.

"There is little I can tell you," he said. "What little I know has come to me chiefly by hearsay. She married an *Americano*. They had one child, a son. The husband and wife separated after a few years. The mother kept the child with her in Mexico, removing to Chihuahua after my family wrested power from the Cabreras. The father left Mexico. Where he went, I do not know, but I understand that his wife continued to receive money from him, which she used for her son's upbringing and education. Then she died. The son was a young man by that time. He left Mexico. There was a rumor that the father had also died and that the son had gone to claim his inheritance, which was supposed to be somewhere in the States and to consist of land."

"Texas land?" Hatfield asked.

"That I do not know, though it might very well be so. The father is supposed to have been a land speculator, and after the war there was a great deal of speculation in Texas land."

"There was," Hatfield agreed thoughtfully. "Well, let's get some sleep. Good night."

"Good night."

Hatfield having set the clock in his mind so that he should awake at midnight, awoke at the time and roused the *don*. They traveled on. . . .

The sun and Hank Wilkins usually rose together. This particular morning was no exception. He had come out of his rude cabin and gone to the one corral his modest layout boasted when he heard the sound of hoofs. He turned in the direction of the sound and saw two horsemen approaching. Hank Wilkins was a horsebreaker and horse trader.

"Early birds," he muttered, "come to catch a few worms mebbe. Nice gait to them hosses, but I reckon I kin match 'em."

Suddenly his gaze became fixed. "No, sir!" he exclaimed.

"I spoke a mite too soon. Dang me iffen I don't know one o' them hosses. If it's the hoss I think it is, I can't match it. No one kin."

As the two riders came closer, Hank Wilkins saw that they were Mexicans. His hand snaked to his hip, came out with his gun. As the riders thundered up, he cried to one of them: "What are you doin' on that hoss!"

"What's the matter, Hank?" the rider on the golden horse drawled. "Don't you know an old friend when you see him?"

"Jim Hatfield! Well, I'll be jiggered! What you doin' in the Mex outfit? Dang me, I almost shot you! I knew dang' well whose hoss it was, an' I knew you'd never sell Goldy. So I jest nachally concluded he was stole. Light, you ol' son an' tell me what brings you here."

Hatfield dismounted, motioned for the *don* to do the same. He introduced the puzzled *Don* Pedro to the horse trader.

"Hank has been in the hoss business ever since I first met him," he said with a grin. "This is his outfit here. Notice the cabin an' the stable. The cabin's about ready to fall apart but the stable's a little palace. Hank takes better care o' his hosses than of himself. Hank always took good care o' hosses."

"Mine an' other people's," Hank said with an answering grin. "In plain words, *Don* Pedro, I used to be a hoss thief, which is what Jim was too kind to say. But Jim here, he saved me from hangin' once an' give me some advice. Don't rustle, he says . . . trade. Some folks think one's about as honest as the other, but I been tradin' ever since. But say, Jim, *you* ain't here to trade. Not Goldy, sartinly not Goldy."

"No, Hank," Hatfield answered. "Reckon you know better than that. I want Goldy changed, an' you're the man to do it. You see I'm a Mexican now, an' I've got reasons fer bein' one. Well, I got the same reason fer wantin' Goldy to look different, too."

"What color you want him?" asked Hank, all business now.

"Reckon black'd be best."

"Reckon so. An' I kin tell by your eyes you're in a hurry. Goldy, do you mind? Do you mind, you four-legged creation o' warm livin' sunlight, if I take the sun off your hide an' make you a black thundercloud for a time? Don't you fret. You'll still be all golden inside. Come along, hoss."

Goldy submitted to being led to the stable. Hank Wilkins had a way with horses.

"Go into the cabin, you two," he called back, "an' rustle yourselves up some breakfast! I don't like fer people to be watchin' me at my work. Go on, go on."

After breakfast, Hatfield and the *don* sat on the cabin stoop and smoked, waiting for Hank Wilkins to emerge from the stable. When he came out with Goldy, Hatfield looked at the animal:

"I wouldn't know him myself," he said as he went to the horse.

"He looks kind o' down," Hank said to him softly, "but that's to be expected. He'll feel better after the dye has dried, which won't take long. Well, what do you think of my work? Ain't he a livin' thunderhead, a black hunk o' shinin' ebony?"

"Yes," Hatfield said. "Yes. Sorry, Goldy, ol' boy. I hated to do it. Hank, do you reckon you could do as fine work on a human as on a hoss?"

"What you mean?"

"Me, my face. Make me look more like a Mexican."

Hank looked at him thoughtfully for a moment. "Reckon so," he said. "I kin give you the right kind o' complexion. A little grease, well rubbed in, follered by a brown dye. I ain't never done that kind o' thing before, but I reckon I kin change you some, your hair fer instance. I couldn't guarantee that your own mother wouldn't know you, but you'd be pretty safe from recognition on the part of folks in general. Come with me."

When Jim presented himself for *Don* Pedro's inspection, the *don* nodded. He swept off his hat in a mock greeting.

"Un hijo legítimo de Méjico," he said, with a bow to Hank Wilkins. "A veritable son of Mexico. Even I would not know you."

"Good," Jim Hatfield said. He held out his hand to Hank. "Thanks."

An hour later he and *Don* Pedro were riding again. Hank Wilkins watched them fade from sight. "I don't know where you're goin' or what you're up to," he muttered, "but I'm wishin' you luck. So long, Goldy. So long, Jim."

Don Pedro Alvarez reached the Circle 7 spread alone—at least Jim Hatfield was not with him. In Hatfield's place, riding by the *don*'s side, was another Mexican mounted on a coal-black horse. To all outward appearances the Ranger had changed his mind about returning to the Angela Mesa.

Sam Morgan was in one of the corrals with his daughter, Texas, and his foreman, Dave Horton, when the two rode up. He was showing his daughter the new horse he had bought for her, growing enthusiastic about it, and in accordance with his nature his enthusiasm ran so high that he did not notice the appearance of the strangers. But Texas noticed them and, waving her hand to them with the free greeting of the West, said: "How do you do." "Thanks, Pa," she said turning to her father, "but we've got company . . . let's come back to the horse later. Did you notice the black horse one of the strangers is riding?"

"Mebbe I kin buy it fer you," her father muttered. More loudly he said: "Light, strangers. You look like you've come a long way. You're jest in time fer dinner."

The two Mexicans entered the corral. "We are looking for Sam Morgan, owner of the Circle Seven *Rancho*," *Don* Pedro said with a bow toward Texas.

"I'm him," Sam Morgan said. "What kin I do fer you?"

"I am Pedro Alvarez, brother of the governor of Coahuila," the *don* answered. "This is my good friend, Felicio Granados."

He paused and seemed to be waiting for something.

"*Señor* Alvarez and his friend are waiting to be introduced to me," Texas said.

"My daughter, Texas," Sam Morgan said, embarrassed. "My foreman, Dave Horton."

Texas held out her hand. The *don* took it, bowed over it, and kissed it. Dave Horton dropped his own hand on seeing this gesture. He replied to the greeting of the Mexicans with a curt nod.

"There goes the dinner bell," he said hastily as the second Mexican was about the repeat the gesture of the first.

Over the dinner, *Don* Pedro explained his mission.

"It's a big deal," Sam Morgan said when he had finished, "an' I'm free to tell you that I'm a mite amazed over the credit part of it. Folks don't usually aim to buy cattle 'less they've got the cash, leastwise that's the way we do business in these parts."

The other Mexican answered in Spanish. "*Don* Pedro's note would be as good as gold . . . silver." *Señor* Granados seemed to place especial emphasis on the last word. *Don* Pedro translated what he had said.

"I don't doubt it," Sam Morgan replied. "I kin see you're a gentleman from the ground up. But, as I say, it's a big deal. I wouldn't aim to swing it alone. Dave, suppose you take a ride over to the Diamond Star and ask Mister Maxwell to pay us a visit. I think he'll be interested in this."

When the foreman had gone, the *don* said with a smile: "He seems to be an excellent young man, that foreman of yours, but a little jealous in his disposition, no? When he returns, *señorita*, perhaps you had better tell him that I have a daughter who is about your age."

"I'll tell him nothing of the kind," Texas flashed, two spots of color glowing in her cheeks. "It's time Dave Horton learned a thing or two. Just because we grew up together is no reason for him to think he owns me. I'm not married to him. . . ."

The *don* smiled at the outburst. "There seems to be a word you have left unspoken in your last sentence, at least your voice seemed to hint of it."

"What is it?"

"The word is *yet*," *Don* Pedro said, smiling almost to himself.

Texas blushed to the roots of her hair and left the table, murmuring some excuse.

"The ways o' women pass the understandin'," Sam Morgan said. "Texas shore does torment that boy. Yet underneath it all, I got a suspicion that he's the one she wants. Only she won't let on to it. You shore got under her skin, *Señor* Alvarez."

"A girl as beautiful as your daughter should have no lack of suitors, I presume," the *don* went on.

"Oh, no, not by a long shot. She could have her pick. I know one mighty fine *hombre*, my friend and neighbor, Orlando Maxwell, who's been doin' a heap o' thinkin' about marriage ever since Texas growed up into a young lady. Not that he's ever mentioned it, but I kin sort o' read between the lines, you might say. Maxwell is rich, richer probably than Dave will ever be. He owns the biggest spread in Texas outside of the Panhandle, an' the only bigger one in the Panhandle is owned by John Holcomb, who I ain't seed in years."

Don Pedro, in discussing the cattle deal, had made no mention of Devil's Pass. Now, hearing the name of the man who had died with his hand in that of his brother, he grew suddenly tense. In a low voice Felicio Granados spoke to him in Spanish.

"Show nothing, say nothing," he said, but Felicio's Granados's own eyes glowed for an instant with the stabbing pain of a memory.

"Let's go set on the porch an' have a smoke," Sam Morgan suggested.

The two Mexicans enjoyed their smokes. Sam Morgan did not know that another kind of smoke was still in their nostrils—the smoke of battle. From their casual air he did not suspect how tired they were.

"Here comes Maxwell," Sam Morgan said suddenly.

Maxwell dismounted and came onto the porch. "Hello, Sam," he greeted. "Dave told me you had some kind of a deal on, so I came right over."

"Where's Dave? Why didn't he come back with you?"

"Dave's out hunting for a mad dog."

"A mad dog."

"Yes, you know that sheep man over to the northeast of my place? Well, his dog went mad and is running loose. I was about to go after him myself when Dave came along. Dave offered to do the job, so I gave him a gun."

Sam Morgan introduced Maxwell to the Mexicans and explained the terms of the cattle deal. "I disagree with your objections to the credit feature, Sam," Maxwell said, when he had finished. "Cash business is old-fashioned. It's time we ranchers learned how to do business on credit. *Señor* Alvarez here is the brother of the governor of Coahuila. As such, I'd be willing to rely on his note in place of cash."

Don Pedro could hardly believe his ears. Jim Hatfield had been right! Jim had said that he could obtain cattle on the Angela Mesa and here were two men who were ready to supply him with them. The *don* looked at Felicio Granados.

Something in his friend's face startled him. It was as though Felicio Granados did not share his delight, it was as though his thoughts were elsewhere, and that he wished *Don* Pedro's thoughts to be elsewhere, too. All at once, for no reason in the world that he could see, *Don* Pedro felt a shiver go up and down his spine. He felt that his friend was trying to tell him something, trying to tell him something with his eyes instead of with his tongue.

"What is it Felicio?" the *don* asked. "You seemed troubled about something."

"I think we should go inside," Felicio Granados replied who could again see a proud, handsome face lying in the depths of the Chisos Mountains. "Business transactions require paper and pens and a flat surface to write on."

His words were interrupted by a faraway shot. *Don* Pedro slumped forward out of his chair.

In a flash Felicio Granados was kneeling beside him. The words he uttered were spoken in a voice too low for the others to hear. "Too late," he was saying. "I should have spoken sooner."

XII

"Where've you been?" Sam Morgan asked Dave Horton upon the latter's return. "An' what are you doin' with that gun?"

"I've been out huntin' a mad dog," Dave Horton replied. "Where's Texas? What's become of your company?"

"Huntin' a mad dog, eh? Sure his name wasn't Alvarez?"

"What's eatin' you, boss? What makes you look at me that way? An' what kind of talk are you talkin'? Mad dog . . . Alvarez . . . what's one got to do with the other?"

"Alvarez has been shot."

"Shot? Why, not . . . ?"

"Gimme that gun."

Dazed, Dave handed the rifle to him. Sam Morgan broke it.

"Fresh fired," he muttered.

"What in hell are you talkin' about, boss? When I left here, Alvarez was eatin' dinner. Now, when I come back, you tell me he's been shot. Crazier yet, you make it sound like you think I shot him. How the hell could I have done that when I wasn't here when it happened?"

"A man doesn't have to be on the spot to shoot a man with a rifle like this."

"You mean you think I shot him at long range? Hell, boss, I couldn't have done that even if I'd've wanted to. I'm not that good, though I'll admit a gun like this could do the trick."

"There's been a bullet fresh-fired from this gun," Sam Morgan said.

"An' I fired it!" Dave Horton cried angrily. "Shore. I admit it. I was out huntin' a mad dog."

"Did you kill the dog, Dave?"

Dave swore fervently. "No. Damned if I didn't spot him over to the east of the Diamond X, but I missed him, an' after that he gave me the slip."

"Then I've got to take you in to jail, Dave. So far it's fer attempted murder, since Alvarez ain't dead yet. I left him upstairs on my bed, unconscious, with his friend and Texas, tryin' to do what little they kin. . . ."

He broke off suddenly. "Pa!" he heard his daughter calling from within the house. "Pa!" The door was flung open and Texas came out, breathless. "Pa," she blurted, "they're gone."

"What? Who's gone?"

"*Señor* Alvarez and his friend."

"Are you crazy, Texas? How . . . ?"

"I don't know. I was downstairs for a few minutes, boiling up some fresh water, and, when I went back upstairs, the room was empty. I don't know what to make of it." For the first time Texas seemed to notice Dave. An expression of fear came into her eyes, mingling with the wonder there. "Dave!" she cried. "You didn't do it, did you?"

" 'Course not, honey." To his amazement Texas was in his arms. "Why, honey," he said unsteadily, "you almost make me glad it happened."

Sam Morgan burst into the house, rushed upstairs, came rushing out again. "She's right! They're gone! I can't make it out. Alvarez. . . ."

"His friend," Texas said, and in her eyes was a queer faraway look. "I think his friend must have been responsible for it. Ever since I first saw him, I've had the feeling that there was something mysterious about him. I've almost felt

178

that I've seen him before."

"I give up," her father said. "Dave, fer the time bein' you're free. I can't hold you fer attempted murder, either, when it comes to that. I reckon I'll be a deputy sheriff all my life without ever makin' an arrest. . . ."

The three of them heard the thunder of hoofs. A tall rider on a coal-black horse was coming toward them at a breakneck pace. He was upon them almost before they knew it.

Paralyzed for that instant, it seemed to them that he was about to ride them down when he swerved. One of his arms shot out, grasped the rifle in Sam Morgan's hands, wrested it from his grasp. Without slackening his mad pace he whirled, completing his reverse, and shot away.

Recovering from his momentary paralysis, Sam Morgan instinctively reached for his six-gun, but Texas seized him by the arm.

"Pa," she cried, "don't shoot!"

By the time he was able to draw, the mad rider was out of range. "Texas," Sam Morgan cried, "that was Granados. Those Mexicans are up to somethin'! What it is I don't know, but their queer goin's-on make me think it ain't on the level. Why didn't you let me shoot, Texas?"

"I don't know," said Texas, and her voice sounded wild. "All I know is that there was something in me that said you shouldn't shoot. Not that man! No, not him!"

They looked at her in wonder.

The rider on the coal-black horse did not slacken his pace. In a short time he overtook another rider moving west across the plain. The two of them galloped side-by-side. They seemed to be heading in the direction of the Comanche reservation.

Felicio Granados spoke quickly. "Saurel, I watched from a distance before acting," he said. "Maxwell's foreman rode up with a message for Maxwell. Maxwell rode off in the direction of Morrow. Saurel headed back toward the Diamond X. Then Dave Horton came back. Sam Morgan talked to him, took the gun away from him. They thought he was the one who had shot you, jest as I figured they would. Then Texas came out. She'd just discovered we were gone. I wanted that gun, so I rode up an' took it. There was no time to do any explainin'. They must still think you were shot in the heart instead o' bein' merely knocked cold with the shock of a bullet fired at a distance from a high-powered rifle, an' that you're more than human somehow. I reckon you ought never to spend that gold piece you had sewn in your shirt."

"I was blind," *Don* Pedro said. "I should have seen. . . ."

"Well, you know now. You know what called me back to the Great Angela Mesa. Anyway, I was kind o' slow myself. I didn't wake up to that mad-dog business till it was almost too late. El Rey de Angeles seems to make a habit o' lettin' other folks do his jobs fer him. In this case he thought he could kill two birds with one stone . . . murder you, an' get rid of a young feller who was kind o' in his way, you might say. He must've done some quick thinkin' to set it goin' like that. But he's beginnin' to make mistakes, he's growin' reckless an' impatient, an' he's takin' long chances. Things haven't been movin' along accordin' to schedule. He's been blocked all along the line, he don't know exactly what to make of it, an' I reckon he might even be gettin' a mite panicky."

"But why didn't you . . . ?"

"Go fer him then an' there? It wasn't the time. There's things to be done, plenty o' them. Fer one thing, your life wasn't safe where you were, which is why I'm takin' you to a place where it will be. Meantime, I'm givin' him rope, enough rope so's he'll hang himself. An' no harm's been done. They can't hold Horton fer your murder when they ain't got your body."

"The gun Horton used. . . ."

"The bullet that hit you didn't come from it. It's true that the bullets in it an' the bullet that stunned you are alike. Did you hear a shot before I joined you? That was me. I shot into the ground an' then dug up the bullet fer comparison. The riflin's on the bullets ain't quite the same. Your bullet is like the one I dug out o' Ned Markham an' out o' my own hide."

The two men had been talking loudly in order to make themselves heard above the hoof beats of their horses, but now they fell silent. The gateway to the Indian reservation came into view; they passed between the sentinel hills, and were soon in the midst of a scene that struck *Don* Pedro dumb with amazement.

The strange method of defense devised by Jim Hatfield so many days before was still in force, but it had been systematized. The work of the reservation was going on, the livestock was being tended, the cornfields were being worked. But while a portion of the women attended to these duties, others sat hunched and silent in a large circle at the center of the reservation, while within that circle their husbands, brothers, fathers slept and ate and talked and smoked and were sick at heart.

"Yes, I know you," was Chief Morning Star's first utterance, after a close look, in response to the question of Felicio Granados. "It is time you have come back." There was a slight tremor in the Indian's voice that cut into the heart of the white man who was facing him. Suddenly the Indian struck himself with both fists upon the chest.

"Oh, Lone Wolf," he cried, his voice resonant with passion and sorrow, "how much longer? You asked and I consented. But there is a limit to what men can bear. My warriors are ashamed, they are sick at heart. They had no hate for the white man but now they are beginning to feel hate, and I am beginning to feel it, too. It is too much! Can we hide behind our women and children forever?"

Hatfield, placing both is hands on the Indian's shoulders, said: "Morning Star, never have Comanche warriors appeared so brave to me as they are at this moment. I have come to tell you that the time is near at hand when the circle that holds them in can vanish, never again to form. Be patient for yet a little longer. Soon this will be over, an' the Comanches will be glad of the noble thing they have done. Will you promise me that, Morning Star? Your words have entered my heart. Let mine enter yours."

The Indian was silent a moment. When he spoke, his voice was low. "When Lone Wolf speaks, I remember my father, who also spoke with a golden tongue. It shall be as you say, for yet a little while longer."

"And will Morning Star receive my friend, to live with him and be guarded by him, for my friend has enemies without who desire his death?"

"Your friend may remain."

XIII

Hatfield rode swiftly toward Morrow. Now that *Don* Pedro was off his hands, he felt free to move again. First, it had been Ned Markham, or rather the mortal remains of Ned Markham, then it had been Bill Evans, finally it had been *Don* Pedro.

Well, Ned Markham was where he had wanted to be, asleep beneath the sod of the only real home he had ever known. Bill Evans was resting up with the Apaches and no doubt recovering under the wise use of their medical lore. And *Don* Pedro was safe with the Comanches.

I've been travelin' heavy, Hatfield thought. *Now I'm travelin' light. From now on I'm goin' to make time.*

He alighted in front of the Wells Fargo office in Morrow, and entered. The same operator who had been there on his previous visit to Morrow was behind the railing of the telegraph alcove. The telegraph apparatus was silent and the operator was lazily sprawled in his chair, sleepily puffing on a corncob pipe.

"Git up an' look alive," Hatfield said.

Astounded at hearing such an order from a Mexican, still more astounded that the order was couched in English with a Texan accent, the operator had to catch the pipe that fell from his suddenly opened mouth.

"Come on," Hatfield said, keeping his voice low. "Move."

The operator went up to him. Hatfield opened and closed his fist, but in that brief instant the operator saw the flash of his Ranger's badge. He swallowed hard.

"What do you want?"

"I want your copies of all outgoin' an' incomin' messages fer the past week."

The operator, troubled, shook his head. "I can't do that," he said, low-voiced. "Leastwise, not without your havin' an order from the court in Austin. You ought to know that."

"I do know it. Austin happens to be three hundred miles away an' I've got no time to go there. Hurry up, before I have to show you the two orders I got hangin' at my sides."

The eyes of the operator suddenly widened in startled understanding. It came to him in a flash when and under what circumstances he had seen this stranger before. That time when he had heard the shooting coming from the Lone Star Saloon—the shooting that he had thought innocent but that he had afterward learned had ended in the death of six men. This man here. . . .

The operator wasted no more time. He produced the messages.

There were only a few. Jim went through them quickly. He tossed all but one back to the operator. The one he retained was in Spanish and translated this said:

Things have gone badly. Am in Marfa.

The message was signed with just the initial **C**.

Hatfield put the message in his pocket, thanked the operator, and went out. His next stop was the Land Office. The sight of his badge gave him access to the records. He spent an hour transcribing them, using paper and pen and ink furnished by the clerk.

An hour later he was back at the Circle 7. Sam Morgan was on the porch, cleaning his gun, when, hearing the clatter of hoofs, he saw once again the Mexican who he knew only as Felicio Granados. This time Texas was not there to stop him. He snapped the gun shut and leveled it at the man who was looking calmly down at him from the height of the coal-black horse.

The Mexican smiled, and the smile was an indication of the fact that he knew the gun wasn't loaded. But Sam Morgan continued to point it, meanwhile shouting to the three men in the last corral, who came running. The noise brought Texas and Dave Horton out of the house. They stopped short in surprise on seeing the Mexican.

"Cover him, boys," Sam Morgan ordered.

A low chuckle came from the Mexican.

Texas stepped forward, looked up at the mounted man. Her breath was coming fast, her eyes were bright.

"I know you," she murmured. "I knew I couldn't be mistaken about this horse."

"You shore have an eye fer hossflesh, miss," Jim Hatfield drawled.

"Holy jumpin' Jimminy!" Sam Morgan ejaculated.

"I told you I'd be back, boss," Jim Hatfield said. "Hello, Vance. I see you got that job I told you to go after."

Vance Thompson's face was awe-struck. "Hello, Hatfield," he managed to murmur.

"I reckon you folks want to know what this is all about," the Ranger said. "Well, I really ain't got time to tell you. I jest rode in here to place this rifle in your keepin'. It's the one I took away from you, Morgan . . . the one that was supposed to have fired the bullet that hit Alvarez. I reckon I ain't wrong in thinkin' that Dave Horton was accused o' doin' it. Well, he didn't do it. I kin tell you that fer certain. As fer all the other mystery about our disappearance, that's simple. We jest whistled up our hosses an' dropped down on 'em from the bedroom window. Alvarez was no more hurt than any *hombre* would be who was punched above the heart. The bullet didn't go into him.

"There's another reason, though, why I came back here. There's still talk in Morrow about goin' fer the Comanches. You've got to see that sech talk stops, Morgan. Get over into Morrow an' tell folks that it's orders . . . *Ranger's orders* . . . that the Comanches are to be left alone . . . that there's a government treaty in force. Also tell them that unless there's an end to this agitation, there'll be a Ranger troop sent to disarm every mother's son in the county. So long, folks. Mebbe I'll be seein' you soon."

"Wait a minute!" Sam Morgan cried. "If Dave didn't shoot Alvarez, who did?"

"I reckon I got a pretty good idea of who it was," Hatfield said. "So long."

In silence they watched him ride away. When he was out of earshot, Dave Horton said to Texas: "Danged if he ain't the only *hombre* that ever made a pretty speech to you without my gettin' angry at him. He shore is some boy. After seein' him, Texas, I really can't see what you see in a *hombre* like me . . . honest."

"Let me be the judge of that, Dave. As for Jim Hatfield, somehow I can't imagine him ever falling in love." Her voice sank. "He seemed so lonely as he rode away. That's what I think he'll always be, lonely, and good, and kind."

"That's it!" her father suddenly cried in high excitement. "Now I know who he is . . . the Lone Wolf. That's him, that's him. You spoke the right word, Texas . . . lonely . . . you gave me the clue."

Out on the prairie a rider talked to his horse. A smile curled the rider's lips and his eyes were a little sad.

"Goldy," he murmured, "or should I call you Blackie now

. . . that's a fine girl back there. She wanted you, an' I reckon mebbe I'd be ready to give you to her . . . if I went along with the hoss. But it ain't in the cards, Goldy. I'd best stop thinkin' o' sech things."

The sadness went out of Jim Hatfield's eyes, grimness took its place, and he rode toward the Diamond X.

The sun was getting low over the western horizon when he entered the ranch house grounds. Smoke was rising from the chimney of the cook house, a sign that the cowpokes would soon be trailing in. One lone rider was adjusting a hackamore on a skittish bronco in one of the corrals when Hatfield rode up.

"Please," he said with a strong Mexican accent, "I weesh see *Señor* Saurel. Veree important."

The cowpoke looked toward the ranch house. Smoke was coming from the kitchen chimney. The cowpoke grinned.

"Reckon you'll find him in the kitchen there, dishin' himself up some o' the boss's extra-fancy grub."

"I see. When the cat ees away, the mice weel play, no? *Muchas gracias.*"

Hatfield went around to the back of the house, opened the kitchen door, and entered. The man at the stove whirled about, startled at the sound of footsteps crossing the threshold.

"You are *Señor* Saurel?" the Mexican asked softly.

"Who the hell are you?" Saurel's hand was on the butt of his gun.

"Please to take hand away from gun," the Mexican said. "I 'ave come long way, from Marfa. I 'ave been sent by *Don* Jaime Cabrera. On the road I 'ave met your *jefe, Don* Orlando. He tell me he 'ave forgot his rifle, the special one, and he ask me to come here to peek it up and breeng eet to him."

As he softly spoke the words, he looked for signs of recognition on Saurel's surly face but there was none. There had always been the chance that Saurel might recognize him, for if Saurel had been able to see *Don* Pedro sitting on Sam Morgan's porch, he must also have been able to see him.

In approaching Saurel so openly, Hatfield had to depend on the fact that to the best of his recollection he had been sitting in the porch's shadows when the shot had come. Now, since Saurel did not recognize him, he saw that such must have been the case.

"What's been happenin' in old Mex?" Saurel snapped irritably, his eyes alert. "The boss got bad news from Marfa. What's it all about?"

"Please, I 'ave not much time. We 'ave suffered a defeat in Coahuila, but all is not lost. That is as much as I can tell you. Now, eef you weel be good enough. . . ."

"All right. Wait here an' I'll bring you the gun."

Saurel came back with the rifle. The Mexican took it from him and fondled it lovingly.

"She ees beautiful," he said. "And she 'ave such a long bright eye." The last reference was to the length of the barrel. "*Don* Orlando 'ave tell me you 'ave keel a man weeth these today. Ah, weeth such a weapon as these, how can a man's aim help but be true."

"It wasn't the gun alone," Saurel cut in jealously. "It was good shootin', that's what it was."

"Oh, I do not weesh to take away any credit," the Mexican hastened to say, "but now I must leave. Perhaps you weel ride weeth me a way. Then I weel not lose time in telling you more about what happened in Coahuila."

Saurel agreed eagerly. As they rode, the Mexican described an imaginary battle. The shadows lengthened on the prairie. Shadows seemed to deepen on the narrator's face, and there was a strange, solemn look in his eyes when he finished. Suddenly he reined in his horse, thus dropping behind Saurel.

"Don't turn around, Saurel!" Hatfield's voice rang out. "I've got you covered. Lift your guns gentle an' let them fall. I'm warnin' you, don't turn around!"

The man in front of him sat for an instant, stiff and dumbfounded, in his saddle. His face was contorted, but the man behind him could only imagine, not see, what it looked like. Slowly he lifted the guns out of their holsters and let them fall.

"Now you kin turn around," said the voice behind him."

Saurel turned, his face twisted in hate and anger. He seemed to be struggling to catch his breath.

"Do you remember me, Saurel?" his captor asked. "Do you remember the face you flung that scalp at?"

"You!" Saurel gasped. "You!"

"Yes, me. Your game's up, Saurel. You've come to the end of the trail. You're through with doin' the dirty work fer a varmint that's even worse than you an' whose game is nearly up, too. Yonder's the settin' sun, Saurel. Your life is a-settin', too. Turn around, Saurel. Git goin'. Ride."

"What . . . what are you goin' to do?" Saurel quavered.

"It's been said that those who live by the sword perish by the sword. In this case it ain't a sword, it's a gun, but it amounts to the same thing. You're goin' to ride, Saurel, into the settin' sun . . . you're goin' to ride hard. I'm givin' you your chance, but I'm tellin' you in advance it ain't much of one. If you think so much o' *your* shootin', you don't know what shootin' is yet. *Git!*"

With a wild cry that was more animal-like than human Nash Saurel drove in his spurs and shot forward.

The man who remained behind waited, gun raised. His horse was a frozen ebony statue. The distance lengthened but still he did not shoot. The fleeing man began to weave his horse. A grim smile curled the lips of the man who watched him.

Hatfield watched the distant rider plunging toward the setting sun. "No, Goldy," he muttered. "I can't do it. That's not the way of the Rangers. But we'll meet again Saurel. Git goin', Goldy! After him, after him! Travel like you never did before."

As he passed the spot where Saurel had dropped his guns, Hatfield swooped down out of his saddle and picked up one of them. Goldy did not slacken his pace. The rider in the distance had disappeared, below the horizon or the roll of the prairie, but, as Goldy let loose a fresh burst of speed, he reappeared.

Gradually the distance that separated the two riders, the one pursued, the other pursuing, was eaten up. Saurel had just begun to believe that he had made good his escape, that by some miracle the death-dealing shot he had expected had not been fired or else had been fired and had missed him, his panic preventing him from hearing the shot, when he heard the sound of hoofs behind him. He cast a frightened glance back, saw that he was being pursued, and dug in his spurs cruelly.

But the speed of Saurel's horse could not equal the speed of the horse carrying the pursuer. He heard the voice of Jim Hatfield roaring down the wind.

"I'm givin' you your chance! No use trying to outdistance me! Slow down an' turn around! If you don't, I'll plug you! You hear me, I'm givin' you your chance! A gun! D'you understand? I'm givin' you a gun!"

The significance of the words broke through Saurel's panic. He could hardly believe his ears, but he understood that unless he obeyed there would be no chance for him at all, whereas if he did, there would be a chance. He drew rein, wheeled his horse. Hatfield thundered toward him. "Catch!" the Ranger roared. "It's your own gun!"

The black object came through the air toward him as the Ranger flashed past. Instinctively his hands leaped up to catch it.

"Now shoot!" the Lone Wolf bellowed without halting Goldy, but curving to Saurel's right in a mad gallop.

Saurel's horse flashed into motion. A cry, hate-filled, broke from Saurel's throat.

"Damn you! I'm sendin' you to hell!"

The six-gun of the foreman bucked and blazed in his hand. Hatfield felt the hot breath of a bullet fan his cheek. Both the Lone Wolf's hands were off the reins now, but neither one of them held a six-gun. It was a rifle they held. The pressure of his knees sent Goldy plunging straight toward Saurel as he brought the rifle stock back against his shoulder, triggered, and blew Saurel's head off.

Dismounting, he looked down at the body. "It was right that you should die from a bullet from this gun," he murmured, "this gun that fired the shot at *Don* Pedro with you pullin' the trigger . . . this gun that I'm sure has done other an' worse things!"

Hatfield returned to the Circle 7.

"Here's the gun that fired that bullet at Alvarez," he said simply. "The man who fired it is dead. This gun killed him. Put it with the other. Now I'd be obliged fer somethin' to eat an' I'll be movin' on."

Sam Morgan was looking at the gun with horror-stricken eyes. He wet his lips. "It's Orlando Maxwell's," he said, his voice coming out of his dry throat in a cracked whisper.

Hatfield, looking down at the palm of his hand, nodded but said nothing. In the palm were four bullets, all alike. One had taken the life of Ned Markham. Another had come out of his own skin. The third had struck *Don* Pedro. And the fourth, still warm, had ended the life of Nash Saurel.

Before Hatfield left, Texas Morgan went to him and gave him her hand. The Lone Wolf looked down softly at the girl standing before him.

"God bless you and keep you safe," she whispered. Suddenly she rose on tiptoe and kissed him quickly on the cheek.

Dave Horton, who was watching, felt no anger. Hatfield burst out of the house, mounted the rested Goldy, and sped away as though the devil were after him. Even after many hours of riding, with the cold night air of the prairie beating against it, the cheek still burned, or so it seemed to Jim Hatfield. He rode all night and the sunrise found him drawing near to the border town of Marfa.

XIV

Hard as Hatfield rode that night, another man had ridden harder. Moreover, that other man had had several hours' start. Orlando Maxwell reached Marfa in the small hours of the morning.

He dismounted before a wooden frame building with a false-front second story. Over the porch hung a sign, invisible in the darkness: **Paul Joliet, Arms and Ammunition.** Maxwell quickly ascended the porch and was about to knock when the door opened.

"Come in," a low voice said.

Maxwell entered, and the door closed behind him. "Come," the voice said. "I have a light and a bottle of whiskey in the back room. We have much to say to each other."

"Where is Joliet, Jaime?" Maxwell asked.

"Circumstances prevent his being here at the moment. I will tell you about that in good time."

On the table in the back room stood a lighted oil lamp and a bottle of whiskey whose contents had already been liberally sampled. The two men sat down. Facing each other, a keen observer would have noted a striking resemblance. But the countenance of Jaime Cabrera, unlike that of his visitor's, was deeply marked by dissipation.

"I received your message," Maxwell said. "What happened?"

"My dear cousin," Jaime Cabrera began, and, although the manner of his speech was thus far polite, it was plain that he was laboring under an inward tumult of angry excitement. "I said in my message that things had gone badly. Your great plan that was supposed to work so well is nothing but rubbish. It was supposed to work so well that, today I should be sitting in the governor's *hacienda* in Coahuila. But, instead, I am here, I am *not* governor, I am still Jaime Cabrera, bandit."

Maxwell sat, tight-lipped, for a moment. He looked at the bottle for a long while before he spoke.

"Generals should not drink," he said at last.

"Bah! Do you think it was that? My men and I fought, and we fought well. We made ourselves masters of the capital, we were prepared to storm the Alvarez *hacienda,* victory was within our grasp. Yes, your plan was perfect. It drew *Don* Pedro and his men up into Texas, just as you said it would. But it did not succeed in keeping them there!"

"Speak plainly," Maxwell snapped, his large black eyes still larger with surprise. "What happened?"

"*Don* Pedro's men returned. How they managed to break through the barrier of Yaquis under my brother's leadership I do not know. You said it would be impossible. Nevertheless it happened. We were driven out of Coahuila, pursued into Chihuahua. I left my men on the other side of the Río and came across, then sent my message for you to join me.

"Yes, cousin"—his voice dripped with sarcasm—"things did not work out according to plan in Mexico. I thought to myself, perhaps my cousin has been more fortunate. Perhaps he has done in Texas what I failed to do in Mexico. If so, then all is not lost. . . ."

He broke off shortly as he saw Orlando Maxwell shake his head.

"What!" he cried. "You have failed . . . too?"

Suddenly Maxwell was on his feet, his face contorted, his eyes blazing down on his cousin. "No!" he exclaimed hoarsely. "I have not failed! Death alone can make me fail!" He fell back into his chair, panting. The flames went out of his eyes, leaving embers there. "The plan," he muttered, and his voice was so low that he seemed to be talking to himself instead of to his cousin, who leaned forward to hear him. "The plan was perfect. It was worked out to the last detail. The worst that could have happened was for one of us to fail . . . you in Mexico, or me in Texas. Then each of us would have had the other to fall back on. For both of us to fail was unthinkable."

"Nevertheless that is what seems to have happened," Jaime Cabrera said softly, the silk of sarcasm still in his voice. "Although you do not say so flatly, I can read between the lines. Tell me, my dear cousin, since this plan of yours was so perfect, and I admit that at one time I thought it was perfect, too, why are you and I now here? Why am I not governor of Coahuila? Why are you not El Rey de Angeles in fact as well as in name? I gladly passed on that name, which was mine by right of inheritance. Such things do not interest me. But I now see that I passed on a thing that is empty of all meaning. What went wrong, cousin? And why do you look at me like that? There is in your eyes a look I have seen in the eyes of men before . . . it is a killer's look. Is it perhaps that you are meditating my death . . . ?" With the words, Jaime Cabrera suddenly had a gun in his hand. Trust is short-lived between fellow plotters.

"Not yours, Jaime," Maxwell said slowly.

"Whose, then?"

"Jaime, do you remember the stranger on the golden horse in Devil's Pass that day?"

"Yes. I remember him because he got away. If we had killed him, I would have forgotten him. But surely. . . ."

"Jaime, that man on the golden horse who escaped from us

that day came to the Angela Mesa in time to prevent the men of the mesa from attacking the Comanches."

"But why did you not kill him?"

"I was not with the attacking party. I did not see the man until he returned to the Circle Seven with Sam Morgan."

"And you recognized him?"

"I did."

"Then why . . . ?"

"There is a time and a place for everything, Jaime . . . killing included."

Jaime Cabrera gave vent to a chuckle without mirth. "Ah, I see, there were ladies present, or should I say a lady? The daughter of Morgan. Well, a king must have his queen."

"Careful, Jaime, or the look which you saw in my eyes and which you correctly recognized may turn out to be for you, after all."

"Your pardon, cousin." Jaime Cabrera stepped back in mock respect.

"I took immediate steps to get rid of this man. Six men led by the outlaw from Arizona, Macklin, attacked him in the Lone Star Saloon in Morrow."

"With what result?"

"He killed all six."

"*¡Ave María purissima!*" Cabrera breathed. "Is it a man you are talking of or a devil?"

"Suffice it to say that he got away a second time. Yet I was to see him once again."

"When was that?"

"Yesterday. Yesterday *Don* Pedro Alvarez came to the Circle Seven."

"*Don* Pedro!"

"Yes and this man was with him."

"And you recognized him for the third time?"

"Not directly. He was dressed as a Mexican and looked like one. But his horse, even though it, too, was disguised, aroused my suspicions. I looked at him more closely. I saw it was the same man."

"Then why did you not then and there . . . ?"

Jaime Cabrera did not finish. Orlando Maxwell was silent as Cabrera gave a short laugh.

"*Sí*, the girl again. Orlando, I warned you from the beginning . . . love and business, they do not mix. You wanted power, you wanted to be a king. All right, I did not say no to it, but you wanted the other as well, you wanted a queen to share the kingdom that was to be yours. As a result, my friend, you have neither."

"I will still have my queen," Maxwell said in a low voice.

"What did you say?"

"I will still have my queen." The dark eyes were filled with an inward glow.

"Are you mad? How can a man have a queen when he has no kingdom? When, at this very moment, even, the law may be looking for him, a thing that is very probable from all that you have told me. For if this stranger could succeed in blocking you at every turn, he probably knows by this time all of our plans."

Orlando Maxwell's eyes were glowing again. "Quiet, Jaime. I did not come to Marfa only to see you."

"What did you come for?"

"For the silver. Where is Paul Joliet?"

A low chuckle came from Jaime Cabrera. "Cousin," he said, "it is plain that the same kind of blood runs in the veins of us both. So you, too, had that idea, eh?"

"What idea?"

"To take back from Joliet the silver we gave him in exchange for furnishing us guns and running them across the

Río. Well, cousin, the silver is ours. There it is, in those chests."

Understanding dawned in Maxwell's face. "What did you do with the body?" he asked in low tones.

"You are sitting on it, cousin," Cabrera said calmly. "Joliet is buried beneath this floor."

"I see," said Maxwell, shortly, nervously. "I see."

"It seemed to be the only thing to do," Cabrera went on, speaking of the murder as though it were nothing. "Of course, if I had won in Coahuila, I might have considered letting Joliet keep the silver we had paid him for furnishing and running the guns across the river. But since the battle was lost in spite of the guns, it was plain that we had nothing to show for all the silver we had paid out. 'The battle has been lost,' I said to myself. 'Shall all that silver be lost, too? No. A victory might have been worth it, but certainly not a defeat. That silver will be much better in our hands than in the hands of Joliet. Who knows? Perhaps, with it, we shall be able to fight again, the second time victoriously.' I did not know, then, that you, too, had failed. Yet, if I had known it, that would have been all the more reason for doing what I did.

"The dream is done, eh, cousin? The parts we were to play, you in Texas, I in Mexico, have not worked out according to plan. We two Cabreras . . . I, the son of my father, and you the son of my father's sister, have not won back the lands of our family, Coahuila, and the Great Angela Mesa. How big a dream it was!" Jaime Cabrera stopped for a moment and looked into space. Then he went on: "It was to be only the beginning. All Mexico was to be conquered, and then a second war with the *gringos*, but this time a victorious one, then the taking back of Texas. And after that, you and I, rulers over what we had conquered and Mexico renamed Terra de Angeles . . . and to you the name of my father, El Rey de Angeles, because the great plan was first born in your brain.

"Ah, cousin, it was a great dream," he added, trying to break the silence of Orlando Maxwell. "Where has it gone? Well, the silver is better than nothing. I came to Joliet, pretending to be interested in buying more guns, and I slipped my knife between his ribs. It was a quick easy death for him, for I found his heart with the first stab. Cousin, would you have done as much for me?"

"You yourself have said that the same kind of blood runs in both of us," Maxwell said. "What you have done for me I would have done for you. You have saved time by doing it first. Attend to what I say now. We must work and work quickly. Get your men across the river as fast as you can. I am going to need them."

"For what?"

"For a cattle drive into Chihuahua . . . my cattle and Sam Morgan's. Texas has grown too hot to hold me but I don't intend to leave Texas empty-handed. But all is not lost . . . far from it. I can still turn my failure into success. If we strike fast . . . but we are wasting time . . . cross the river and bring your men over. On second thought, no. Bring over enough men to transport the silver." Orlando Maxwell's brows knitted as he visualized his plans, then he went on. "We will cross back and move down the river on the other side. It will be faster and less dangerous. Then we can strike north to my ranch, move down on the Circle Seven, do our job there, and be in Chihuahua before any effective force can be organized to stop us." Maxwell's voice sank. "And she will be with me," he murmured. "She will be with me."

When Jim Hatfield reached Marfa, he found his quarry gone.

XV

The sun moved up the heavens, then down again, and sank in the west. The stars came out. The moon sent its mild light down upon the earth. Once more the morning star appeared. And beneath the sun, beneath the moon and the stars, beneath the morning star, men rode, many men. Behind them, on a tireless black horse whose true coat was golden, rode a single man. He was like a hound following a trail still warm with animal and human sweat, still fresh with the marks of hoofs.

The morning star faded. The sky in the east lightened. The sun came up. And Texas Morgan and her father came out on the east porch of their ranch house. Looking toward the east, both saw it at the same time—dust rising.

"Large party o' horsemen comin' this way," Sam Morgan said. "Hold on now, what's that?"

They saw a smaller cloud of smoke somewhat in the van of the larger cloud. A single horse and rider became visible.

"Why, it's Dave!" Texas cried.

"An' he's ridin' like the devil was after him. Look thar. He's bein' shot at."

Puffs of white smoke were rising behind the lonely rider. They heard the distant sound of shots an instant later.

"Get into the house, Texas," Sam Morgan ordered. "I'm thinkin' it's Injuns. God, an' to think I sent all the men out on the range last night because so many of the cows were calvin'. Get into the house, Texas! Get the guns ready! Meantime, I'll set the cook shed afire. Maybe it'll be seen an' we'll git help."

Dave Horton thundered up and dismounted. "Into the house!" he cried. "It's Maxwell. I was over near his west range when I spotted them roundin' up all Maxwell's cattle . . . Mexicans. But Maxwell's leadin' 'em. They sighted me but I jest managed to get the start of them. I know what he's come for, Texas! He's come for *you!*"

There was no time for Sam Morgan to light his fire. They had barely time to get into the house and bolt all the doors. Looking out the windows, they saw that the ranch house was surrounded.

Suddenly there was the sound of shattering glass. Something hard landed on the floor near Sam Morgan's feet. He stooped and picked it up. It was a stone with a piece of paper wrapped around it.

He peeled it off and read what was on it. His face purpled with a sudden rush of blood.

"It's to you, Texas," he said, and his voice sounded strangled. It read:

Come out, and come out alone. If you do, the ranch and your father's life will be spared. Otherwise, the Circle 7 will be put to the torch.

"It's in Orlando's . . . in Maxwell's handwriting. God, I can't believe it."

Texas took the note from him. Her face was very pale. Dave Horton, looking at her with agony in his eyes, saw that she had come to a swift decision.

"No!" he cried, and her father echoed his cry.

"There's nothing else to do," Texas said, making an effort to keep her voice steady. "We can't possibly stand them off. If I go out to him, at least you and Dave and the ranch will be safe. And I'll be alive. Otherwise . . . well, you read what the note says."

"Orlando Maxwell, my friend," Sam Morgan murmured.

"He was never your friend, Dad. You can see that now."

"No!" her father cried again. "I won't let you do it, Texas. Oh, I've known that he wanted to marry you, he told me so. But I told him that it was up to you."

"He never asked me because he knew I would say no. Now he means to take me by force. There's no choice, Dad. If I don't go out to him, the three of us will die. Do you need any-thing else now to convince you that Orlando Maxwell was behind the burning of those ranches, and God knows what else? You doubted it up to the last, but you can't doubt it any longer. Would a man like that stop at anything to gain his ends?"

Texas Morgan's question went unanswered.

"Isn't it better for me to take my chances on going with him than for all of us to die here? A woman can see into a man's heart, Dad, better than any man can. I know what's in Orlando Maxwell's heart. After all that's happened, I know. If he can't have me, he won't let anyone else have me. And to prevent anyone else's having me, he's even prepared to kill me, to kill us all. I've got to go out there, Dad."

"Let me go out!" Dave Horton cried suddenly. "He tried to get me once, and failed. Let him succeed this time. With me out of the way, maybe he'll call his Mexicans off. Maybe he'll give you time to think it over, Texas, and in the mean-time help might come."

Texas Morgan smiled through her tears. "You want to go out there and get killed for me. You think that would help me. Oh, Dave, do you think I would want to go on living with you dead?" The last exclamation seemed wrung from her heart.

"She's right, Dave," her father said gruffly. "Maxwell has

got us roped, tied, and branded." A stifled sob broke from his heaving chest. "Texas, I reckon. . . ." He broke off, unable to speak further, finding her in his arms."

Dave Horton was looking out the window. "Maxwell's keeping well out of sight," he muttered. "If I could only spot him."

"Dave," Texas was beside him, "I've got to go out to him."

He nodded, like a man dazed.

"But I won't say good bye to you, Dave. I'll get away from him. I'll come back to you."

"Texas, Texas." His tones were full of despair.

Her face seemed to grow even paler. She turned from him and walked toward the door.

The lonely rider on the black horse whose true color was golden—the lonely rider who yesterday's sun had seen following a trail like a hound, upon whom the stars and the moon had looked down to see him still following that trail, who the morning star had greeted—what had become of him? Where was he, now that he was most needed?

The sentinel hills of the Comanche reservation saw him that morning. They saw him as he shot by between them and as he sped like a black comet toward the center of the reservation. On he came, toward the magic circle of women and children, where Morning Star and the braves were waiting. Now he had come to break that circle and deliver Morning Star and his braves from their long ordeal of shame.

The women and children, the chief and his warriors, saw him coming, so did *Don* Pedro, and a cry broke from him. Then a great chorus rode to greet Jim Hatfield as he came on. The women and children made a path for him. Like a thunderbolt he burst into the circle. His voice welled out to

Morning Star: "Red brother, arise! Arise and mount your horse! Let all your warriors rise and mount! Your ordeal is over! You are done with hiding behind your women and children. Long have you waited, with a wonderful patience, for me to come to you with these welcome words. The moment has come at last! Arise, and follow me!"

"Where?" Morning Star shouted.

"Into battle!"

At the words, the face of the chief became transfigured with a spasm of joy. Orders leaped from his lips. The warriors made a rush for the rifles that had been stacked within the circle. Each warrior, after obtaining his weapon, sought out his own horse. In quick time every one of them was mounted and ready. *Don* Pedro rode up to Hatfield. "Where to?" he asked tensely.

"The Circle Seven. They're in trouble."

Orlando Maxwell's Mexicans, ranged in a circle about the Circle 7 ranch house, heard an oncoming sound that chilled their blood. It was the war whoop of the Comanches. Texas Morgan, opening the door and stepping out on the porch to give herself up, heard it, too. Through the open door, Sam Morgan and Dave Horton heard it. They felt the hair rising on their heads.

For an instant they stood there paralyzed, looking at each other. Then, each rushed out of the house to protect Texas. The girl stood transfixed, gazing toward the oncoming horsemen. She became aware of the two men beside her.

"It's he," she breathed. "It's he! Look!"

But they had already seen the man on the black horse.

The Mexicans broke before the attack of the Comanches. Their panic, which had begun when they had first heard the blood-curdling sound of the war whoop, flamed into frightened life as the guns of the Comanches began to speak and they saw their comrades toppling from their saddles.

Dave Horton threw Texas to the porch floor and covered her with his body. Moving shapes flitted past the porch, went around and around the house. Horses shrieked their death agony. The Mexicans, trapped, strove vainly to break through the outer circle that rimmed their own circle in. Driven back toward the house, they found that the Comanches had broken through to form a moving inner circle that kept them from making the house their refuge.

Don Pedro, his horse shot from under him, suddenly found himself face to face with a figure that was also on foot. In the moment he had before the figure leaped upon him with drawn knife, he gave a shout of recognition. It was Jaime Cabrera, the last of the Cabreras, the hereditary enemy of his house.

A shout came simultaneously from the hot throat of Jaime Cabrera—he had recognized Alvarez. The two men closed. *Don* Pedro seized the swiftly descending wrist, jerked the lower half of his body back to escape the other's murderous kick. Jaime Cabrera's face was contorted with an expression that was almost joyful.

"We are well met, Alvarez," he gasped. "I die happy if I can take you to hell along with me, son of a cursed breed."

But *Don* Pedro, desperately maintaining his hold on the wrist, made a last despairing effort. He jerked the wrist down, swung his body behind the other, and bore Jaime Cabrera to the ground beneath his weight. He heard a low gurgle; the figure beneath him relaxed, and lay still. The last of the Cabreras was dead.

About to rise, *Don* Pedro threw himself flat across the body again. A horse and rider, looming up, gigantic and terrible, hurtled over him. It was Orlando Maxwell, the light of madness in his eyes, as he made for the ranch house porch. He had seen the three huddled figures, the golden hair of Texas Morgan. All the rage and hate born of shattered dreams and frustrated hopes flamed up in him in one concentrated blast at the sight. The mad lust to kill drove him forward, carrying death in both hands.

But a shape dashed athwart his path, a hatless rider on a black horse, and Orlando Maxwell saw in that terrible instant the man who almost single-handedly had smashed his plan and kept him from kingship. His lips curled back from his teeth. A wild shout came tearing up out of his throat, his guns blazed.

But Jim Hatfield, who in the thick of battle had never left off looking for one man and only one, had at last caught up with Maxwell. He did not let hate blind his eyes. He came in bent low, his own guns blazing, and sent one bullet speeding into Maxwell's brain, another into his heart.

"You kin get up now!" he shouted. "We've got 'em on the run!"

The three figures on the porch, rising to their knees, saw him point with his gun to a body on the ground, then dash off. They heard his voice ring out and order that the cattle be rounded up and the Mexicans let go.

They came off the porch, looked down at the body of Orlando Maxwell. They saw the remaining Mexicans fleeing toward all four points of the horizon, some of the Comanches in hot pursuit, other busy with the cattle. They saw Jim Hatfield come back, driving pack horses ahead of him. He dismounted before them, swayed slightly, steadied himself against Goldy. Horton, old man Morgan, and Texas looked at him without speaking, marvel in their eyes. *Don* Pedro walked over to them.

"The last of the Cabreras is dead," he said to Hatfield,

"dead by his own knife. Those who live by the sword perish by the sword."

Hatfield nodded. "That makes it a clean sweep," he said. "Maxwell is dead, too. His cattle now belong to you. And the silver, it's here, on these horses. It belongs to John Holcomb's kin, whoever they are." He turned to the others. "I suppose you're wonderin' how I got here. It's simple enough.

"When I reached Marfa, I found Maxwell and Cabrera gone. I nosed around a bit and decided to investigate the abode of a certain Joliet, dealer in arms an' ammunition. I found Joliet dead and buried in his own shop, and saw where chests had been opened an' their contents taken an' loaded on horses outside. The trail took me across the Río. Goldy wasn't too fresh, but we managed to hang on the trail from then on. The fact that Maxwell had to take time to round up his cattle gave me the extra time I needed.

"Maxwell knew his game was up in Texas, but I figured he wouldn't leave Texas without at least makin' an attempt to take somethin' besides the cattle an' silver along with him. I don't have to tell you what that was, Miss Texas. Seein' that was the fact, it was plumb logical to play the card I'd been holdin' in reserve fer some sech contingency as that . . . namely, the Comanches."

"Hatfield," Sam Morgan said gruffly, "when they made you, the mold was broke."

"There's things to be done," Hatfield said. "There's men to be buried, not alone here but in other places. Over in the Chisos Mountains, in Devil's Pass there are bones of honest men waitin' to be put in a common grave. There's legal matters to be straightened out, sech as dividin' Maxwell's land, an' givin' back title to the ranchers who were burned out. There's got to be a proper ceremony when the Comanches take possession of the extra land the government has given 'em by treaty . . . an' there's got to be a proper ceremony fer the Apaches, too."

"But you're tired," Texas Morgan burst out. "You've got to rest. You've done so much already, so unbelievably much, more than it seems possible that any one man could have done. Why can't you rest, why can't you leave all these other details to others?"

"I'm here, Miss Texas," Hatfield answered, "an' bein' as I'm here, I reckon I got to finish my job clean. As fer my bein' tired, I reckon Goldy here is a heap more tired than me. I'd like him to rest while I'm attendin' to these matters. An' then him an' me will be gettin' back home."

She came close to him, stood on tiptoe, and her lips once again brushed his cheek. At the same time he felt his hand clasped by Dave Horton.

Hatfield's bleak smile spread across his lips and he turned to search Maxwell's body. It revealed several things of interest. There was a locket suspended from a gold chain and worn next to his skin. Opening it, Hatfield saw a picture of a woman and a child.

His ma, he thought, *an' him when he was a baby.*

There was also a letter from the mother, written to Maxwell some twenty-five years back when the latter had been away at college. It said in part:

My son, never forget that you are a Mexican. Never forget that the lands now lived upon by strangers and by aliens once belonged to your family. Think of this when you go to bed at night and when you awaken in the morning. Think, plan, dream, how the land may once again be ruled over by men in whom flows the ancient aristocratic blood of the Cabreras.

By a strange freak of chance, a little of that land is about to become yours. Your father, without knowing that the land once was ours, had purchased some range on the Great Angela Mesa in Texas. Word has come to me that your father has died and left the land to you. It is like a sign, an omen, that *all* the land that was once ours, will be ours again—will be *yours,* my son.

At present the land is being worked by men hired by your father, but when you have finished with your education, you will go there and I shall come to join you.

She died before she could keep that promise, Hatfield thought. Further search revealed several sheets of paper covered with a fine handwriting. It was Maxwell's plan of campaign, worked out in detail. Several names appeared in it, and Hatfield recognized two of them as belonging to outlaws who were wanted in Arizona. He thought it probable that he had killed both of them, either in the Lone Star Saloon, or perhaps even on that terrible day when he had broken out of Devil's Pass. Hatfield read on, oblivious of the others. When he had finished, he thought: *Such a big dream, an' there he is now, a hole in his heart an' his plan blown out of his skull.*

A week later Jim Hatfield returned to the Carson Ranger station and reported in full to Captain McDowell. The stern old captain, listening attentively, felt his heart swell with pride as the recital came from Hatfield's lips. A softness came into his eyes which he strove in vain to conceal.

"I reckon I'd've got to Maxwell sooner," Hatfield said, "if all of these other things hadn't sort o' slowed me up an' taken me here an' there over so much territory. Anyway, that attack in the Lone Star was why I came back to the Circle Seven as Felicio Granados. I figured that whoever had tried to get me the first time, would try it again if I was recognized.

"So on my way back with *Don* Pedro I looked up Hank Wilkins in Del Río. You remember him . . . the ex-hoss-thief I saved from hangin' once an' who ever since has traded in hosses legitimate, if you kin call a horse trader legitimate. Well, there ain't no one who kin do with hosses what Hank Wilkins kin do. He made Goldy over fer me.

"I reckon that's all, Cap'n. The Angela Mesa is at peace. It's an almighty sweet land down there, an almighty sweet land. There was a curse on it fer a time, the curse of Orlando Maxwell's evil dream. He wanted two things, that *hombre* . . . power an' a girl . . . an' to get them he was ready to stop at nothing. But he's gone now, an' the curse is lifted."

"An' Jim Hatfield did the liftin'," the gruff captain said. "You seem a mite sad in the eyes . . . 'specially when you speak o' what an almighty sweet land you left behind. Was the land the only thing you left behind, Jim? Seems to me there was mention in your report of a Miss Texas Morgan."

Jim Hatfield looked at him with level eyes. "I reckon I'm tired, Cap'n," he said slowly.

A look of amazement came into Captain McDowell's face. "The world's comin' to an end," he breathed. "For the first time since I've known him, Jim Hatfield has admitted to feelin' tired. Well, I'll be jiggered."

The Lone Wolf grinned. "I reckon it wasn't so much what I did," he said, "the ridin' an' the fightin'. I reckon I ought to be used to such things. I reckon what's got me to feelin' a mite tuckered is all the anxiety that went with this job, the stoppin' o' things before they started, wonderin' whether Mornin' Star could keep his warriors under control, wonderin' if Bill Evans was all right with the Apaches, bein' in one place when I felt I was needed in another."

"Jim," said Captain McDowell decisively, "I'm goin' to let you have a vacation. How long do you want?"

" 'Bout an hour," Hatfield said. "Long enough fer me to curry Goldy before linin' up with the rest o' the boys fer the sunset flag lowering."

The captain burst into a roar of laughter. "Jim, you shore had me fooled fer a minute. I shore enough thought you were aimin' to ask fer a furlough."

"Reckon I wouldn't know what to do with it if I got one," Hatfield said.

Captain McDowell's face became serious. "Well, in that case . . . ," he drawled, picking up a telegram from the desk.

Jim Hatfield did not let him finish. "I understand hell has sort o' busted loose up in the oil country," he said, "an' honest folks are callin' fer help."

"How the devil d'you know that!" Captain McDowell burst out in amazement.

Hatfield grinned and pointed to the telegram. "It was no trick to read that," he said, "even if the letters were upside down."

The Lone Wolf, mounted on his golden horse, rode again to bring law and order, peace and safety to those who deserved them and death to forces of evil at work in the north. As Hatfield rode north, the glory of the Texas Rangers rode with him.

About the Author

Leslie Scott was born in Lewisburg, West Virginia. During the Great War, he joined the French Foreign Legion and spent four years in the trenches. In the 1920s he worked as a mining engineer and bridge builder in the western American states and in China before settling in New York. A barroom discussion in 1934 with Leo Margulies, who was managing editor for Standard Magazines, prompted Scott to try writing fiction. He went on to create two of the most notable series characters in Western pulp magazines. In 1936, when Standard Magazines launched *Texas Rangers*, Scott, under the house name of Jackson Cole, created Jim Hatfield, Texas Ranger, a character whose popularity was so great with readers that this magazine featuring his adventures lasted until 1958. When others eventually began contributing Jim Hatfield stories, Scott created another Texas Ranger hero, Walt Slade, better known as El Halcón, The Hawk, whose exploits were regularly featured in *Thrilling Western*. In the 1950s Scott moved quickly into writing book-length adventures about both Jim Hatfield and Walt Slade in long series of original paperback Westerns. At the same time, however, Scott was also doing some of his best work in hard cover Westerns published by Arcadia House, thoughtful, well-constructed stories, with engaging characters and authentic settings and situations. Among the best of these are *Silver City* (1953), *Longhorn Empire* (1954), *The Trail Builders* (1956), and *Blood on the Río Grande* (1959). In these hardcover Westerns, many of which have never been reprinted, Scott proved himself highly capable of writing traditional Western stories with characters who have sufficient depth to change in the course of the narrative and with a degree of authenticity and historical accuracy absent from many of his series stories. *Lone Star Brand* will be his next **Five Star Western**.